DOCTOR WHO

THE STAR BEAST

THE CHANGING FACE OF DOCTOR WHO
The cover illustration of this book portrays the Fourteenth DOCTOR WHO,
whose physical appearance mysteriously resembled that of his tenth
incarnation

THE STAR BEAST

Based on the BBC television adventure
The Star Beast by Russell T Davies
from a story by Pat Mills and Dave Gibbons

GARY RUSSELL

BOOKS

BBC Books, an imprint of Ebury Publishing
20 Vauxhall Bridge Road
London SW1V 2SA

BBC Books is part of the Penguin Random House group of companies whose
addresses can be found at global.penguinrandomhouse.com

Penguin
Random House
UK

Novelisation copyright © Gary Russell 2023
Original script copyright © Russell T Davies 2023
from a story by Pat Mills and Dave Gibbons

Doctor Who is produced in Wales by Bad Wolf
with BBC Studios Productions.

Executive Producers: Russell T Davies, Julie Gardner,
Jane Tranter, Phil Collinson & Joel Collins

First published by BBC Books in 2023

www.penguin.co.uk

A CIP catalogue record for this book is available from the British Library
ISBN 9781785948459

Editorial Director: Albert DePetrillo
Project Editor: Steve Cole
Cover Design: Two Associates
Cover illustration: Anthony Dry

Typeset by Rocket Editorial Ltd
Printed and bound in Great Britain by Clays Ltd, Elcograf S.p.A.

The authorised representative in the EEA is Penguin Random House Ireland,
Morrison Chambers, 32 Nassau Street, Dublin D02 YH68

Contents

Gary Russell would like to give special thanks to:
Steve Cole; Anthony Dry; Paul Simpson; Martin
Geraghty; Dave Gibbons; Gary Gillatt; Scott
Handcock; Pat Mills; Paul Neary; Mark B Oliver;
James Page; Mick Schubert; Dez Skinn; John Wagner;
and of course my amazing former boss,
Russell T Davies, without whom ...

1
The Hunt

Stew Ferguson pulled the collar of his coat up round his neck and shivered, as he walked through the night on his way to his overnight cleaning job at the Steelworks. Weird thing was, it hadn't been cold a few seconds ago, but, as he'd passed Blackcastle Passage just now, a gust of wind had whipped around him and surprised him. Okay, Camden at the start of winter was never the warmest part of London at the best of times, but that had been a very sudden blast of icy air.

Stew realised it had faded away, and he tentatively pulled his collar back down, peering up Blackcastle Passage, a small mews-like walkway which led to the back entrances to many of the shops that ranged along the main street.

He was quite surprised to see a tall, thin guy in a long blue coat, hands in pockets, whistling to himself, strolling towards him, his brown hair blowing slightly in the breeze.

Odder still, Stew thought, was that massive blue box behind him. Stew could normally see the back doors of the shoe shop from this angle, but tonight that weird blue box was in the way.

Stew thought it looked familiar, and then it hit him. His granddad had been a copper back after the war and his mum used to have a photo of him on the mantelpiece, standing outside a box like that. They used to be called police boxes. Surely no one made police boxes any more, so what was this one doing there?

'That your box, mate?' he found himself asking the thin man.

'I'm sorry,' said the man, his voice betraying his most likely south London origins. 'Oh that box? No, that box, nothing to do with me. Oh no.' Then he threw a look directly back down the passage at the box. 'Because if that was my box, it wouldn't have just kicked me out. It wouldn't have dumped me here and locked its doors without so much as a—' The man stopped as he realised Stew was gaping at him. 'Sorry, I tend to go on a bit.'

Stew had a sudden feeling of – what did they call it? – déjà vu. Had he met this bloke before, maybe working at the steelworks? Nah, so maybe he'd been a customer back in his milkround days. There's was something tickling on the tip of Stew's mind about him. Oh well...

'You all right mate?' Stew asked.

'Yeah, fine, no problem.'

Stew smiled. 'Missus kicked you out, yeah? My ex did that once. My mate Billy says—'

The stranger didn't seem to be listening, and instead just interrupted Stew's train of thought. 'Oh, I'm in London.' He flicked his tongue out a couple of times, like a lizard. 'Tastes like the twenty-first century.' He looked over at a shop. It was empty, boarded up, but Stew could still see the name on a faded sign above the door. Megabyte City.

'Went out of business donkeys' years ago,' Stew said to the stranger. 'That time all them planets appeared in the sky.' Stew sighed. 'Lost my job that day, you know. I was a milkman back then and—'

'Planets? In the sky?' The stranger seemed very dismissive.

'One of those "It Never Happened" lot, are you? Well, it did happen,' Stew said angrily. 'Cost me everything. Lots of people died and—'

The stranger suddenly touched Stew's arm. 'It's all right,' he said softly. 'It was a long time ago.'

And Stew felt curiously relaxed. He smiled. 'Yeah, yeah, it was. Right, anyway mate, gotta get off to work now.'

And feeling relaxed … no, really, really relaxed, for the first time in, well, as long as he could remember, Stew Ferguson felt good. Tonight's shift would be okay, he reckoned. Yeah, nothing could upset him now.

And Stew wandered off, whistling. He hadn't done that in years either…

As the man left, the Doctor shoved his hands back into his coat pockets and, with one last wistful look back at his TARDIS, stepped out into the busy street.

Things had been … weird. That was probably the best word. Then again, it always was after his body had gone through that strange metamorphosis his people called regeneration. One minute he'd been a blonde woman, standing on a clifftop, the next, bang, a flash of golden regeneration energy and he'd become a tall, gangly man.

Okay, normally, the body would be completely new, but this time, he'd found himself back in an earlier one, a bit like putting on a favourite shirt or comfortable old shoes. Nevertheless, it was unusual and not at all what he'd expected.

But, frankly, the whys and wherefores of that could wait for another day. Right now, he wondered where the TARDIS had brought him.

He sniffed. Definitely London, definitely early 21st century – ozone in the air, cabbages in his nostrils, grime already on his fingertips. A large sign attached to a tube station told him he was in Camden. The Doctor liked Camden. Always good shopping in Camden Lock, though probably not at 6.30 at night, going by the clock in that shop window. Another turn of a corner and whoa, yes, people. Even more people. People were great. People were fun. And these were crowds of people – at 6:30, in the dark – so it was late in the year. November probably, there was a chill and a dampness in the atmosphere. The Doctor smiled. Oh, how he loved London. He loved people. He loved crowds. He loved—

Someone knocked into him.

'Hello,' the Doctor said, but they just carried on, staring at the ground as Londoners tended to do. Eye contact, he remembered seemed to be a no-no in London. He recalled once getting on a London bus. He'd said hello to the driver, who didn't do anything but grunt. He had sat down next to a nice lady with a bit of shopping. She'd shuffled her shopping aside so he could sit better. He had thanked her and then started talking about the weather

4

(Londoners always talk about the weather) and the awful traffic (another popular subject) and then he started explaining where he was going. And the lady had stood up to get off, without saying a word back. Except she hadn't got off at all, she'd just moved to another seat near the back of the bus. The Doctor had looked at her in surprise, but she wouldn't catch his eye. Why were humans in cities so anti-eye-contact? Eyes were wonderful things, windows to the soul and all that—

'Hi there,' he said as a young child crashed into his side, but she too hurried on.

'Whoops,' he said to a young man with a pushchair as it crashed into the back of his legs, nearly knocking him down. 'No, we don't do that, do we ...' But the man, the pushchair and the piles of shopping bags in said pushchair had already been swallowed up by the crowd.

The Doctor realised that maybe this close to Christmas wasn't the best chance he'd get of a jolly, happy conversation out of random strangers.

'Ahh, well,' he said to no one in particular.

He jiggled his jaw again. It still seemed strange that he'd got the voice, face and body of an earlier version of himself. He was pretty sure that hadn't happened before. Somewhere in the back of his freshly regenerated mind was something about the Gallifreyan Laws of Time but before he could focus on that, the memory got swallowed up. Like his brain was saying to him, 'Stop trying to understand why you've taken on an old body out for a spin again. Just enjoy it, cos you quite liked it last time. And you did say you didn't want to go, and—'

The Doctor closed his eyes for a second, pushing the thoughts aside, and letting London move around him rather than him move around London.

Deep breath.

Eyes open.

Smile on.

And – oh, that person staggering towards him, with an absurdly high pile of four carboard boxes in their arms, each box decreasing in size as they went up, was going to crash into him. After all, they simply couldn't see where they were going. Which was very silly but slightly endearing too.

Awww, he loved humans.

'Hold on,' he said, walking towards the person with the boxes, which he noticed were starting to topple. 'Let me help.'

And he took the top box off and placed it on the bonnet of a car conveniently parked beside him.

As the person stopped, all the Doctor could see was red hair.

He took the second box off and now he could see the face.

It was a woman's face.

A slightly frustrated woman's face.

Hang on …

He knew that face. Especially when it was all scrunchy and grouchy and frustrated like that.

And he almost laughed with the shock of realisation, until he felt the stab of fear that came with it.

'Thank you very much,' said the woman sarcastically. 'Not helping.'

The Doctor replaced the top box, hiding the top of the woman's head so that neither of them could see anything of the other.

'Oi! D'you mind?'

But the Doctor did mind. This woman meant the world to him and it burned that he couldn't just sweep her up in the biggest hug.

But no, it couldn't be her. There wasn't that much coincidence in the universe … was there? He moved the top two boxes again.

Yup. It was her.

'If you've finished playing games, mate!'

Donna. Donna Noble.

Donna who, if she recognised him, would die, her mind obliterated by the after-effects of a two-way human/Time Lord biological metacrisis. Donna, the most important woman in creation. Donna standing there after saving the universe from the Daleks by deactivating their reality bomb. Donna operating the Daleks' magnetron to send twenty-six planets home. Donna in the TARDIS, starting to break, her mind being swamped by her copy of the Doctor's, threatening to override her own, filling it with too much information. Donna repeating the phrase 'Binary, binary, binary,' unable to break the cycle. Donna who, if she ever remembered him – or Jack, or Ood, or Davros, or Martha, or Hath, or Rose or time beetles or any of it …

Hang on.

Donna hadn't recognised him.

He stared, but no: there was nothing there, not even a slight hesitation.

7

She shuffled the boxes slightly, letting the small ones covering her face drop into her crooked arms so she could speak to him. 'These aren't mine,' she explained. 'It's all hers.'

She jerked her head to her left where someone noticeably wasn't.

It seemed that Donna had only realised she was alone at this precise moment. 'Where is she?' She looked at the Doctor, that familiar accusatory look. 'I said, where is she?'

The Doctor didn't speak. He didn't dare. Not just for fear of sparking a metacrisis resurgence but more importantly because that tone in Donna's voice always made him feel like a 10-year-old who'd been caught with his hand in the biscuit tin.

Awww, how he'd missed Donna Noble.

But no, he had to get away as soon as possible, just in case.

And Donna yelled out one word that guaranteed the Doctor was going nowhere.

'Rose?' she bellowed.

'What?' gasped the Doctor.

'Rose!'

'What?' he said again, fractionally louder this time, looking around. Surely Rose Tyler couldn't be here as well. Not in this universe. Not in this time.

'ROSE!'

At least three people who might have been called Rose looked at Donna just in case this mad woman with boxes, in a cheap black jacket and daring sweater with different

8

shades of red stripes across it, actually did want their attention.

But no, a new voice answered with a sighed, 'Cooooming.'

And now at Donna's side was a teenaged girl.

'Sorry, Mum,' Rose was saying, 'but I had to pop back. I needed to buy a bag of eyes.'

Mum? Did she say Mum?

And then the Doctor twigged. Rose was Donna's daughter. Good name. She appeared to be a very nice 15-year-old – he chose the notion of 'nice' based solely on the fact that, unlike her mother, Rose wasn't shouting, and her face wasn't scrunchy or grouchy. But oh goodness, he could see Donna's fierce intelligence in those eyes. And the face. Although the fact that she was wearing a nice simple green T-shirt under a denim jacket and a flowered skirt meant she had some fashion sense, which Donna had never had, so she must've got that from her dad. Shaun, that was his name. Shaun Temple, Donna's husband. Last time the Doctor had seen them together was at their wedding – he hadn't dared go inside, but he'd seen Donna's temperamental mum Sylvia and Donna's wonderful and amazing granddad Wilf there. And he'd given them a wedding gift to pass on to Donna, a lottery ticket. A lottery ticket that would set Donna and Shaun, and by default Sylvia and Wilf, up for life. It was the only time he'd ever seen Sylvia smile at him.

Hang on, he thought.

'A bag of eyes?' the Doctor repeated.

The girl, Rose, held up a small plastic bag of Googly Eyes, the kind that could be stuck to anything and, if you made whatever they were stuck to move, the eyes wobbled twice as much.

Cute.

Donna passed her boxes to the Doctor, who took them as if this was a perfectly normal thing to do. 'She's got this online business,' Donna explained to him. Then she turned to her daughter. 'But you should really spend your evenings doing your homework, not fiddling about and posting things to Dubai.'

Rose's attention, however, was fixed on the Doctor, which he found uncomfortable. Maybe eye contact wasn't all it was cracked up to be after all. She was staring at him. No, more than that, it was like she was staring into him, like—

'Who are you?' she asked him.

'Hello, Rose, it's so nice to meet you.' The Doctor slowly placed the boxes on the ground. Time to retreat, stop this conversation before it could properly start. But then he felt his jaw moving and heard words coming out that he was pretty sure he hadn't okayed with his brain. 'My name is …'

He needn't have worried. Because before his mouth could finish its apparently autonomous statement, a massive flash lit up the night sky, accompanied by a sonic boom that drew everyone's attention away from whatever they were doing and up towards the darkness above.

Well, everyone except Donna Noble who chose that moment to bend down to retrieve her packages, and begin emptying them out, transferring the contents more evenly into just two boxes.

10

Something was rocketing across the sky. Behind it, a ring of rainbow clouds had appeared, almost like the fronds of a nebula. A gateway had been opened, and this something had shot through it and was now plummeting downwards – faster than things should normally plummet out of the sky.

Donna was babbling away over her boxes of fake fur, wholly unaware of the drama above her. 'I said to the man in the shop this was wrong. I mean, I took one look at him and remembered that you should never trust a man with a goatee, and he was like, "Oh, I know better" and I said, "Mate", and …'

Rose shook her mum's shoulder. 'Mum, there's a plane crashing!'

But Donna didn't hear her properly. 'Yes, I said to him. But Rose, watch and learn how to pack correctly.'

'Mum,' Rose insisted. 'The plane!'

'I don't think that's a plane …' the Doctor muttered. He glanced around – everyone other than Donna and Rose was ghoulishly filming the forthcoming crash on their mobiles. Good. No one could see him as, from the pocket of the suit, the Doctor produced his sonic screwdriver and drew a square in mid-air, which immediately became a 3D display showing the plummeting spacecraft up against the sky. 'Interesting …'

'How did you do that?' asked Rose.

'D'you know, I'm not entirely sure.' He tapped at the bottom-right area of the screen and pinched with his fingers. Immediately the image changed and they could see the spacecraft close up. It was long and glittering-

11

blue, but ruptured down the side, smoke billowing out of it.

'That's a spaceship!' Rose breathed.

'It's a spaceship in trouble,' the Doctor declared.

'Mum!' Rose said to Donna. 'It's a spaceship!'

But Donna was still sorting boxes, checking the weight of bits of fur and rearranging everything. 'Yes, of course it's a spaceship,' she said absent-mindedly. 'There's a spaceship crashing on London right now.' Donna shook her head sadly. 'You're worse than your great-granddad.'

Rose's great-granddad? thought the Doctor. That would be …

Wilf! Lovely, brilliant Wilf. The Doctor couldn't help himself, he looked at Donna. 'Your granddad! Is he—?'

But Rose interrupted, still staring at the Doctor's floating screen. 'It's gonna crash!'

She was right. All the people in the street gave a slightly odd 'Oooooh' as if they were watching a New Year's Eve fireworks display, when in fact they were seeing a massive fireball erupt upwards as the spaceship made contact surprisingly close by.

The Doctor nodded to himself. A big explosion and yet no real crash of impact, London still stood. He wondered what fuelled this spaceship to have caused so little damage. He decided it would be a good idea to find out the answer to that question.

He tapped the sonic screen and it just disappeared. He needn't have worried about being caught on camera with impossible tech; with the show effectively over, camera phones were down, and people were already heading back to their cafés or the tube entrance or whatever else they were doing.

In the middle of this, Donna finally stood up with her perfectly rearranged and repacked boxes, stuffing the ones she no longer needed into a council recycling bin. 'There now, that's better. Time we were off.'

Me too, thought the Doctor, eyeing the column of smoke from the crash site billowing on the skyline.

Rose sighed in frustration. 'Mum, how'd you do this? How do you always manage to miss everything?'

Donna smiled at her. 'Cos I've got better things to do.' She glanced back at the Doctor. 'Nice to meet you.' Then she leaned in a bit closer. 'Word to the wise, though: you can wear a suit that tight up to the age of thirty-five. And no further.'

The Doctor turned from her scrutiny, frowning as he touched his waist, his hips, his chest. His relationship with age was an interesting one, after so many regenerations. He looked in a café window – yup, he looked older than last time he'd this face. Not by much, but there was just an extra laughter line or two around the eyes. And, yeah, he needed a shave too by the look of it.

He wished he knew why he'd taken this face and body again. Was meeting Donna today just another coincidence, or could he somehow have selected this body in preparation for this very encounter?

Donna was already walking away from him, still utterly unaware they knew one another, thank goodness, still with her brain and mind and body intact. But Rose? Rose was staring at him again.

'How did you do ...?' and she made the shape of the screen in the air.

He smiled at her. 'I just did,' he replied without replying at all.

She smiled back, like they had a shared a secret between them. And then she was gone, after Donna.

He watched them for a second, still thinking about Donna. Brilliant, clever, amazing Donna. And the old days, when she had saved the entire universe. And he smiled sadly. No one would ever know. No one could ever know.

'Rose!'

The Doctor swung round. Now what?

Facing him was a London black taxi cab. Leaning out of it, a man, probably early fifties, big grin on his face. The Doctor recognised him. And understood why he was repeatedly yelling for the out-of-earshot Rose.

Shaun Temple, Donna's husband and Rose's dad. *Perfect!* thought the Doctor. Shaun had exactly what he needed.

'Taxi!' he yelled and walked towards the cab's open window. He was about to speak when Shaun slammed his hand down hard on the horn, making the Doctor start.

'That's my daughter over there, mate,' Shaun said. 'And my missus. Hoped I'd be in time to pick them up.'

'Yes, that's lovely for you,' the Doctor said, 'But I need a cab urgently. I need to go north, towards that explosion. Something crashed, you see. Can you get me there?'

With a sigh at the direction taken by the now out-of-sight Donna and Rose, Shaun tapped his mobile in a cradle on the dashboard. 'Satnav says they're closing all the roads.'

The Doctor leaned in, conspiratorially, exaggerating his London accent even more. 'Oh, I know some routes that even taxi drivers don't, trust me.' He reached into his inside jacket pocket and brought out his psychic paper. 'Grand Master of "the Knowledge".'

Shaun frowned. 'It says Grand Mistress.'

The Doctor smacked the psychic paper against the cab and muttered, 'Oh, catch up.' Then he smiled again at Shaun. 'C'mon, let's go.' He opened the cab door and let himself into the back. 'Allons-y.'

Hadn't said that in a while, he reckoned, almost missing Shaun's cheeky French retort of 'Oui, oui, Monsieur.'

The taxi moved off. The Doctor gave a couple of 'left here' and 'If you take a right up there, we can cut through' type commands which Shaun duly followed. Presumably he'd been convinced by that brag about the Knowledge, the test all London cabbies had to take to prove they knew the name and location of every street in London and the shortest route to get there – which, to be fair, the Doctor did, even the ones not marked on any map. He checked that Shaun's Hackney Cab licence ID was visible, took a deep breath, then spoke. 'So, you're, umm, Shaun Temple, right? Which means that woman back in Camden, your wife, that's … Donna, right?'

Shaun nodded. 'Yup. How'd you know that?'

The Doctor thought quickly and a name popped into his head, from the old days. 'I know a friend of hers. Nerys.'

Shaun laughed. 'Oh, that Nerys. How is she?'

The Doctor hadn't expected that. 'Oh, fine,' he replied as noncommittally as possible.

'Since the accident,' continued Shaun.

'Nah, not that fine,' the Doctor said casually.

'Well,' Shaun said, taking a turn rather too sharply. 'Well, it was her fault.'

'Fined,' the Doctor opted for. 'She's been fined. For the accident. That was her fault.' Change the subject, Doctor. 'Nerys was saying about you and Donna and … she must be Donna Temple now?'

Shaun laughed. 'Nah, mate. She's still Donna Noble. She refused to be Noble-Temple cos she says it—'

'Sounds like an old ruin,' the Doctor ended the sentence.

'That's her,' Shaun laughed. 'And Rose Noble too. I was never gonna win that battle, was I? But I don't mind. I've got the best two girls in the world, mate.'

Move on, Doctor, move on. He leaned a bit closer to Shaun's ear as the taxi narrowly avoided clumping a dumpster outside a hairdressers. 'But Nerys said something about a lottery win or … something.'

Shaun shook his head. 'Oh, Nerys and her big mouth, that was supposed to be a secret. Cos you know what happened, right? Can you guess?'

'I can't guess,' said the Doctor because he really couldn't.

'Donna happened. She gave it all away. To charity.'

'All of it?' The Doctor could remember how much it was. It was … a lot of money.

'Every single penny, mate. Well, we bought a house,

that's the one thing we did first.' Shaun laughed again. 'And you know what? We can't afford to run it! How mad is that? And do I complain? No, mate, I do not. That's the greatest love story, isn't it?'

'Probably, yeah,' agreed the Doctor, thinking Shaun needed to be sainted.

'Me, putting up with all that. I'm a saint.'

'My thoughts exactly,' the Doctor agreed. 'So, she gave all your money away?'

'Triple rollover. One hundred and sixty-six million quid.'

The Doctor winced at the thought of it. Not that money meant anything to him, but to the Nobles…

'Next left,' he suddenly said, and then sat back in his seat with a sigh. 'Why did she do that?' he asked himself. Then grinned. 'Because she's Donna Noble, of course.'

MINISTRY OF DEFENCE

Military Command Secretariat
SDC
Devesham
Oxfordshire

Our Ref: FOI2023/964128

Dear Ms P Carter

Thank you for your email dated 30 November requesting files concerning the following information:

'The November 2023 UFO incident (full) at Millson Wagner Steelworks (Camden) Ltd'

I am treating your correspondence as being a request for information under the Freedom of Information Act 2000 (FOIA) on behalf of the science pages of The Observer periodical.

We have completed a search of all paperwork (inc: mechanical and electronic) records and I can confirm that the MoD does hold some information but there is a question as to whether it falls under the scope of your request.

There was an incident at the above-mentioned industrial site near Camden, of that there can be little doubt as it was witnessed and recorded by many members of the public and therefore is in the public domain. This means it falls under Sections 21(1) and 21(2) of the FOIA.

However, the FOIA does not cover the release of potentially sensitive documents revealing what, if anything, is known of the object that struck the site and its resultant whereabouts.

Under Section 16 of the FOIA, the Space Defence Centre and the combined military units that operate from here, and to which the SDC answer, are not at liberty to divulge whether the object was of military (domestic or foreign) origin. Therefore at this time, it does not fall under our jurisdiction to provide any further details.

As you know, the Government issued a Level 8 DSMA on our behalf regarding this incident. We would respectfully both ask you to acknowledge that, and also remind you that you – as a member of the NUJ – and your newspaper are not permitted to request any further information pertaining to this incident until either twenty-five (25) years have passed or the Government of the day declares the reports accessible to the FOIA, whichever happens sooner.

I am sorry that I cannot aid you any further.

Yours sincerely

W Buckland CBE
Director, SDC

2
The Star Beast

Stew Ferguson was in hiding. He hadn't meant to hide but things were moving at a colossal speed and he really didn't know what else to do.

He had turned up at work on time – not something he could always claim, to be fair. Tommo the security guard had let him in through the security fence before heading home, probably via the Oxford for a pint or three. Stew wasn't Tommo's biggest fan, always complaining about the left, the right, the kids, the old people and everything like that. The type of bloke who'd probably paid for a blue tick on Twitter. But now he'd gone, wandered away, leaving Stew to gaze at his place of employment.

The steelworks itself took up the square footage of a typical football pitch, but, if you added in the perimeter fence and small industrial roadways, it was probably twice that again.

It had been set up late last century, amidst a certain amount of opposition from the locals, who weren't happy at a massive industrial plant being built in the heart of Highgate, just a stone's throw from the bottom of the Hampstead flatwood. But the owners had assured everyone that the chimneys were clean and no noxious fumes or noise would ever affect them. And, to Millson Wagner's credit, they'd been true to their word.

So this evening, just as he did every evening, five days a week, Stew had walked through the exposed-to-the-elements areas of the steelworks, then up a couple of the metal ladders until he reached the enclosed office area on the third floor. Just inside the corridor was a cupboard where the vacuum cleaner was kept along with various brooms, black bags and a couple of squeezy bottles of chemicals that were probably dodgily out of date.

Getting these out, he dragged them into the small open-plan office and began wiping down the tabletops, carefully moving a couple of mugs that one or two of the younger guys who worked there always failed to wash and put away. Not in Stew's job description to clean those. Stew wouldn't describe himself as a jobsworth, but there were limits.

Then there was the office where Mr Keith worked – he was the site manager and oversaw everything that went on. Smelting, transport, collection, waste removal. Stew knew from conversations he'd had with old Keith that it was quite a tricky balancing act keeping a business like Millson Wagner (Camden) Steelworks running smoothly.

Stew liked old Keith, he'd been a customer in Stew's milkman days. He'd been very generous last Christmas and Stew was hoping he might get another bonus this year.

He was still thinking about that when he heard the noise. It started like a whine and at first Stew wondered if some machinery outside in the actual machine areas had been left on. But no, it was getting louder. As Stew looked out of the office window, he saw what looked like an aeroplane dropping towards the steelworks – and he was right in its path.

It all happened so fast. Rooted to the spot, Stew could see the sparks, the flames and the smoke coming out of the plane. Death was approaching.

And then something weird happened.

The plane hit the steelworks but it didn't really explode. Instead, the steelworks did, a massive orange ball of flame shooting upwards to light up the sky. The office windows blew inwards, and Stew dived to the floor as fragments of safety glass showered all around.

After a few seconds, Stew realised he'd been holding his breath and he let it out in a few shuddering gasps. He unclenched his fists, noticing he'd dug his nails right into his palms, and thought maybe he should go and see if anyone needed any help.

He staggered out of the office area and into the dark night.

Right at the centre of the steelworks, positioned in the furnace area, was a tall, cobalt-blue structure. It was surrounded by hunks of twisted metal and concrete, and there was a big hole down one side from which steam and smoke was spluttering. But beyond that, there really wasn't any major structural damage. The thing looked like some sort of giant rocket pointing upwards, as if aimed at the heart of the huge blast furnace, as if it had flipped 180 degrees seconds before landing. How?

Molten steel from the huge vats above was spilling down to the ground, sending splatters of white-hot liquid everywhere. Stew watched as some of the nightshifters walked carefully towards the craft in their protective suits, raising their hands to ward off the incredible heat. As he looked again at the hole in the side, he could see where the metal had ripped outwards. Nothing had *hit* this thing. Something had burst *out*. From inside.

And it finally occurred to Stew that this wasn't any sort of human aircraft. Somehow, he just knew it was alien. Like those planets in the sky from fifteen years back, all over again.

Stew did the only rational thing he could think to do. He ran down the steps and out of the main building, towards Tommo's security hut by the fence and hid inside it.

Within moments, he heard the screech of heavy-duty brakes, quickly followed by slamming doors and shouting voices.

Blimey, Stew thought, *it's the army. They were quick.*

He peeped out through the window and took in the scene. Land Rovers. Some large trucks. A couple of ambulances too. He hoped none of the nightshifters were hurt.

No police cars, mind.

There was something about the military men and women, though: they didn't look like ordinary army people, like you see on the telly. They were all very smart, in tough black fatigues, with shoulders, arms and legs and the tops of their chests covered in shiny black armour. They wore military helmets with the visors down, and carried attack rifles. As one passed the hut, he could see the chestplate was emblazoned with an insignia – UNIT. He didn't know what that meant. Probably some special SAS-types.

One guy was yelling out orders like he owned the place. Stew caught a glimpse of him as the man's visor was up: youngish, Chinese by the look of it. The Land Rover he was standing next to had that word UNIT on it too.

Stew ducked as a torch beam swiped around and he could sense it hovering on the window of Tommo's hut before moving elsewhere. Stew wasn't sure why he was scared of these people. They were the army; surely they were the good guys? But something told him he ought to stay out of sight for now.

He raised his head just enough that he could see a little bit, hoping no more torch lights would come his way.

'I want a Red Perimeter,' the Chinese guy in charge was yelling. 'Access to the south-east only. Now move!'

Stew frowned at something else which caught his eye. Surely that wasn't a military vehicle?

It was a black taxicab, parked up some way away from the military guys. Maybe it had brought a journalist here or something. Stew wondered if the cab might be his best way out of all this – make a dash for it once the soldiers had all gone through the perimeter fence and—

A man jumped out of the taxi. Long blue coat. Tall, thin … Hang on, that was the bloke he'd spoken to back near Camden Lock! What was *he* doing here?

Stew ducked back down, trying to gather his thoughts. Could the bloke he'd met before be a journalist? That might explain his skulking around earlier. Stew decided he'd try and get out in a moment, contact him and—

Damn! Where had the guy gone? The taxi had already left.

Then, the door to the hut was wrenched open and the thin man in the blue coat was there.

'Hello again,' he said with a big infectious grin. He pulled the door shut behind him and sat on the floor next to Stew. 'Having fun?'

Stew shook his head. 'Not really, mate. I just want to go home.'

'Don't blame you. I'm the Doctor. What are you doing here?'

'I'm the cleaner.'

'So were you inside when it all happened?'

Stew realised the Doctor was whispering. He clearly didn't want the army types to find him either.

'Yeah, saw it all.'

'Are you okay?' the Doctor asked.

After a moment, Stew nodded. Somehow he felt that he was. This guy had a way of making him feel relaxed. 'I just need to get away from here, tell my mate Billy MacPherson about all this. He won't believe me.'

'Why not?'

'He'll have slept through it all.'

The Doctor seemed to drift for a moment, as if something was on his mind. 'Tell me about it. I've got a mate just like that. She misses all the fun.' Then he glanced back outside. 'Now, quickly, tell me *everything...*'

Not too far away was an area of north London known locally as the flatwood, a large area of scrubland around which a whole suburb had grown up.

This part of north London had been heavily damaged during the Blitz, that terrible period of the Second World War when great swathes of the city were razed in the early 1940s. After the war, new buildings were constructed, new roads and new transport hubs swelled, but the flatwood itself was left abandoned and overgrown. It soon became a popular play area for children, and, nearly eighty years later, it was still exactly the same, although, back in the 1970s, the local council had at least put up some half-hearted swings and a roundabout for the kids to play on. A crude football pitch existed at the centre of the flatwood and one entire side of the scrubland was lined by poplar trees.

Behind these trees was a short alleyway, full of wheelie bins, running along the back gardens of the inhabitants of one of those terraced post-war streets, Bachelor Road.

Bachelor Road was, to the casual observer, a fairly unremarkable street, lived in by fairly unremarkable people, leading happy but unremarkable lives.

However, that casual observer would be very, very wrong.

Number 23 Bachelor Road was a very special house indeed, lived in by some very special people. The fact that they didn't draw attention to themselves was just an indication that, as yet, they didn't realise just how special they were.

Over the next few hours, that was about to change for ever.

Right now, two of those apparently unremarkable people were walking along Bachelor Road, heading home.

Donna and Rose Noble, having jumped off the tube at East Finchley, were lugging their two boxes home, one each. They were having a laugh about something they'd seen at the cinema a couple of nights ago, when Rose noticeably slowed down. It took Donna a second to realise her daughter wasn't immediately beside her, and she glanced back at Rose, then followed her eyeline forward.

Three teenage lads on bikes were weaving their way down Bachelor Road towards them, not completely recognisable in the dark night, but clearly Rose knew who they were.

As they slowed down, the one at the front yelled out, 'Oi, Jason, you all right?'

The second one followed up with a 'Looking good, Jason', whilst the third one just gave out an unpleasant cackle and wolf whistle.

The lead one steered towards Rose. 'Give us a kiss, Jay Boy!' and then shot off, followed by the other two, all of them laughing.

Rose stood there for a second, took a deep breath, and then began walking forward, throwing a smile at her mum, as if nothing had happened.

But Donna was seething. 'I will get them …' she started,

but Rose just grabbed her arm and led her towards the door of number 23, handing over her box as she got the front door key out of her denim jacket pocket.

Donna was still staring after the lads on their bikes. 'Is that Josie Wingate's boy?' she snapped. 'Callum or whatever he's called?'

'Just leave it,' Rose said by way of an answer, and opened the door, stepping across the threshold.

'No, I'm gonna tell her, cos I remember she had lots of names at school and I should know, I invented them and—'

To shut her up, Rose reached back and dragged her mum inside and closed the door. Slowly. Carefully. Deliberately not making a big deal out of any of it.

She then took all the boxes from Donna and walked down the thin hallway towards the back, where the house opened out into a large kitchen, with a small dining area beyond that.

And a back door to the enclosed garden beyond.

Rose's safe space.

Donna was hanging her coat up in the hallway when she saw a figure standing in the kitchen looking at them both. 'Oh, more trouble,' Donna said caustically. 'I should never have given *you* a key.'

The object of Donna's scorn was currently standing over the cooktop, adding spices to a huge saucepan of tuna madras. This was Sylvia Noble, Donna's mother, resplendent in a navy-blue smock and black jeans, a dishcloth flung over her shoulder.

If you'd said to Sylvia twenty years ago, 'Do you consider yourself a strong and powerful woman?' she'd have just laughed and said, 'Perhaps. Possibly. Maybe. Never thought about it.'

But since then, Sylvia's life had been turned upside down. And back up again. And upside down again. And …

She and her husband, Geoff, and their only daughter, Donna, had lived a quiet life in a nice part of Chiswick. Donna had been engaged to a man called Lance Bennett who she and Geoff were … okay with, although Geoff always reckoned that Lance treated Donna like she was his pet rather than his equal. And whilst Sylvia might have pointed out once or twice, back then, that being equal to her daughter might involve Lance lowering his own standards, Geoff was fiercely protective of his daughter.

Lance had disappeared on their wedding day and Donna had never been able to explain what had happened.

Then Eileen, Sylvia's mum, had passed away and her dad, Wilfred, had needed somewhere to live, so she and Geoff and Donna had bought a bigger house up on Wessex Avenue so Wilf could move in. Dad at the time was making a few quid by running a newspaper stand near the school at Park Vale. But after a bunch of boys set it alight one Sunday morning simply because he sold copies of the *Muslim News* and *Emel* magazine, Wilf chucked it all in and retired to focus his energies on his allotment and his telescope. (He was an honorary member of the Royal Planetary Society. Sylvia was dead proud of that.)

It had been Geoff's allotment originally but when he

died very suddenly, Dad felt he had to honour his son-in-law by keeping it going. Truth be told, Sylvia reckoned he kept it in better shape, and certainly grew better potatoes and runner beans than dear Geoff had managed.

Then the strange things had begun happening: little alien blobs of fat falling out of people, the ATMOS things in cars going mad, the planets in the sky and then, of course, those awful Dalek things that had nearly killed her and Dad before dragging the whole world across the universe. All of these had involved Donna's 'friend', the Doctor. Frankly, Sylvia didn't really understand the Doctor, who he was or what he did. Dad adored him, but Sylvia found him irresponsible, selfish and deserving of every slap round the chops she had given him, and probably a few more.

He had turned up one night in the rain with Donna. Her daughter was out of it completely – the Doctor explained as best he could, and Dad seemed to get the gist of it. All Sylvia knew was that the Doctor had done something to Donna that had cost her all her memories, all her experiences with him. Despite Sylvia knowing those things were dangerous and probably frightening, she had to concede the Doctor had brought something good, no great, out of her daughter for the first time.

And it was all gone as a result of whatever had happened up there, in outer space.

So, for the past fifteen years, ever since the wedding to lovely Shaun, ever since the arrival of their own child, Sylvia had done as the Doctor had begged: to keep Donna away from everything that could be linked back to

31

him. Space aliens. Weird happenings. Sci-fi movies were banned as much as possible. Dad had even thrown out a copy of a book by that disgraced industrialist Joshua Naismith, despite the fact Donna had given it to him.

And they'd had to go through the house, through Donna's things, even through Facebook – Wilf had got his friend Netty, god rest her soul, to do that – and remove all traces of Lance Bennett from Donna's past. Just in case…

Sylvia had babysat at various points while Donna tried to get a job, showing the baby every episode of *Lovejoy*, hoping they too could be shielded from all that spacey nonsense by falling in love with antiques and detectives.

Donna, however, hadn't been able to keep a job. Sylvia felt awful because she moaned and complained about this lack of success, but of course knew the real reason was that something inside her daughter's soul had been taken away for ever. Of course, Sylvia could never let Donna know, so she had to maintain this pretence that she still thought of her as wilfully lazy and incompetent.

For Sylvia, every time she saw Donna she felt a wave of sadness at what had been lost.

In her head, Donna was still her little girl.

That little girl who, aged two, used to come into her and Geoff's bed every morning for a cuddle. The little girl who one night had woken up at about 11pm, not realising it wasn't the morning and wandered in to snuggle with her parents only to find they weren't there and, convinced she'd been abandoned, began sobbing such deep traumatic sounds that Sylvia and Geoff had run upstairs, terrified of what had happened to create this primal howling from their daughter.

The little girl who, aged 10, had left Sylvia in Tesco's because she had spotted a small boy standing in an aisle, distressed because he'd lost his own mummy. Donna had walked him all over the store until she had reunited the boy with his equally distraught mum and won a special award from the manager. And got her photo in the *Herald*'s Little Heroes section.

The teenager who had snuck out of home one night with Veena and gone to some club in the city called Taboo and snuck home the following morning.

And now, all these years later, the daughter with whom she clashed all the time. Every single waspish comment that they made to one another, every time one of them stomped out of whichever home they were arguing in, just tore open the scar on Sylvia's wounded heart.

How much she wanted to tell Donna the truth, to tell her she had been brilliant, she had saved the entire universe. But instead, she had to play the harpy, the nagging, ungrateful, selfish mum. Because if she didn't, Donna's brain would burn and she would die. In agony.

And Sylvia hated herself for it.

But good god, she hated the Doctor even more. And swore to Wilf that if that man ever turned up again, she'd smack him so hard that she'd knock him into next week – time traveller or not.

'I've made you a nice curry,' Sylvia said as Rose headed towards the back door.

Donna sighed. 'You didn't need to. We've still got that

33

giant sausage roll from last Thursday.' She shook her head at Sylvia. 'I don't need my own personal food bank. It's not my fault I lost my job … All right, that actually *is* my fault, but still.'

Sylvia couldn't help herself. 'If you'd kept some of that money …' she started and immediately regretted it.

The money. A wedding gift from the Doctor, although he'd explained that really it had been a gift from Geoff, in some convoluted time-travel way involving a pound coin of his; Dad had claimed to understand but not Sylvia. Point was, Donna and Shaun had millions.

And then they didn't. Because Donna was Donna.

Every time Sylvia brought it up, she regretted it because it was another potential trigger.

Rose, who had witnessed many arguments triggered by the words 'money', 'lottery' and 'squandered', stepped in to distract them both.

'Gran, did you see that spaceship? Was it on the news?'

Sylvia's heart froze for a second. A spaceship? 'No, I didn't,' she snapped more aggressively than she'd intended, especially to Rose. 'I mean, I won't … I couldn't … oh, how many times, there's no such things as spaceships.' She looked at Donna, who was sticking her finger in the tuna madras. 'You didn't see anything did you?'

Donna sucked her finger and shook her head. 'You know me, Mum. I'm Dumbo, I miss everything.'

No sign of brain burning out. Sylvia relaxed a fraction. 'Well, good. Cos it's nonsense.' To change the subject, Sylvia leaned over and kissed Rose on the cheek. 'You look absolutely gorgeous,' she smiled at her granddaughter.

Rose just grinned widely, her whole face lighting up at the compliment, and showed Sylvia the boxes.

'Just gonna put these in the shed.'

As Rose started to move away, Donna turned from the curry and held her daughter's face in her palms, looking her squarely in the eyes. 'I would burn down the world for you, darling. I hope you know that. If anyone has a go, I will be there. And you know what? I. Will. *Descend*…'

Donna let go and opened the back door for Rose. With a huge smile of joy at her mum, Rose scampered off into the garden.

Sylvia looked down towards the old rickety faded blue shed, Rose's workshop, with a huge KEEP OUT sign on the side, and that funny chimney that didn't work. Wilf had started to build it for her, but never finished, so in the end Donna had taken over. Donna, who could barely hold a hammer let alone hit a nail straight. But she and Rose had built it together, painted it, even set up the light that automatically came on when you opened the door. It probably wasn't the greatest shed in the world, but it was watertight, hadn't fallen down in any storms and, most importantly, it was their special thing.

'What was that all about?' Sylvia asked Donna.

'Boys from school.' Donna's face momentarily contorted in anger. 'Callum bloody Wingate.'

Sylvia nodded silently. As Donna put the kettle on for a cuppa, Sylvia returned to stirring the curry. 'I never know … when I say she looks gorgeous, is that right? Is that sexist? Cos I never said it when he was … oh …' She

35

couldn't express what she wanted to say. 'Sorry. You know what I mean.'

Donna might almost have been smiling. 'Does she look gorgeous? Yes. So stop worrying.'

Sylvia's mind was full of memories. Jumbled together. Months, no *years*, of therapists and doctors and voice lessons and hormone treatments and learning pronouns and … and a … 'I just get clumsy,' she said finally.

'I know,' Donna said quietly. 'So do I, but that's what happens.' And she and Sylvia were finally looking at one another directly, keeping eye contact. 'You have a kid,' Donna went on with a slight smile. 'You think, good, I've got this, that's mine. But then she grows up into this extraordinary, beautiful thing and you think where the hell did she come from? How lucky am I?' And the smile faded from her face. 'Don't *you*, Mum?'

And Sylvia knew she'd been thrown a bone. 'Oh yes, *definitely*,' and found she was actually smiling as she returned to the curry.

'I wish,' muttered Donna and she crossed to the kitchen table and opened up her laptop, with its weird Formica-patterned cover which Shaun had spent many weeks finding for her on the internet. 'Look Mum, I'm job-hunting, just for you.'

A minute or two passed when no one said anything; Sylvia cooking, not wanting to start another job-related argument while Donna searched on the internet. Then Sylvia froze as Donna spoke again.

'Funny that spaceship thing. D'you remember, Gramps used to talk about flying saucers and—'

'Now don't start all that, I've said there's no such thing.' Having shut down the conversation as quickly as she could, Sylvia changed the subject. 'Oh, did I tell you, I saw Susie Mair? She's looking a lot better. Shorter, obviously, but then again—'

'And then he stopped,' Donna broke in. 'He used to talk about aliens and UFOs and little green men from Mars – and then he stopped. Never mentioned them again. Round about the time … the time I forgot everything.'

And Sylvia's heart broke. Donna's face was a picture of pure pain and every maternal instinct in Sylvia cried out to hold her. Hug her, tell her everything. Anything to make that expression on her face go away.

Instead, she stirred the curry again. 'Long time ago, darling,' she said with painfully practised dismissiveness. 'Fifteen years.'

But Donna was not letting this go. 'I just wish I knew what happened. There's this … gap …'

Sylvia could have cried. Instead she took a deep breath and shrugged, not catching her daughter's confused eyes. 'There's no great mystery. You had a little bit of a breakdown, sweetheart.' She smiled hopefully at Donna. 'And then you got better.'

Donna nodded. 'I know. But I'm so … stupid!'

'Don't!' Sylvia snapped, totally aware of the hypocrisy in what she was about to say. 'Don't *ever* say that.'

'I am, though,' Donna sighed. 'I keep losing job after job because … sometimes I think there's something actually missing inside me. Like I had something lovely. And it's gone.' Donna was staring down the garden now, at Rose's little shed. 'I kind of look to the side, like something should be there and it's not. And I know, I've got Rose, and Shaun. And you. And … and the biggest sausage roll I've ever seen, frankly.' And she was back staring at Sylvia. 'I should be happy, Mum. I should be really happy. But some nights, I lie in bed, thinking what have I lost …?'

Not for the first time, nor she suspected for the last, Sylvia Noble could say absolutely nothing helpful, reassuring or honest to her own beloved daughter.

And it absolutely killed her.

The alleyway that ran along the back of the Bachelor Road houses and led up to the flatwood was, for this time of night, unusually crowded: it had two whole people in it, both standing next to the wheelie bins, upon which Rose had placed the cardboard boxes she and Donna had brought back from Camden. Recycling day was tomorrow.

Next to Rose, bubbling with an excitement he usually reserved for the latest Insta by Funkanometry, was Rose's 10-year-old friend, Cholan 'Fudge' Mirchandani, who lived in the house opposite.

'Have you seen?' Fudge said, waving his mobile phone at Rose, but so vigorously that she had no chance to actually see what the news report on it that he wanted her to see. 'On the flatwood? A spaceship's landed!' His eyes were huge through his glasses, full of enthusiasm and joy.

Rose smiled and raised his slightly-too-big red baseball cap a few centimetres up so she could see his face better. 'Fudge, that was miles away not—'

38

Fudge wasn't giving up. 'No, a bit fell off. Like an escape pod. Shazza texted, she reckons there are aliens inside.'

Before Rose could say anything about his story, or for that matter Sharon Allen's typically hysterical texting, Fudge was running up the alleyway towards the flatwood.

Rose paused for a second, then shrugged and pelted off after him.

As she reached the end of the alleyway, she could see Fudge had stopped on the scrubland. A fairly large group of adults and kids were already there, phones out, taking photos and texting friends. A couple of policemen were rather feebly and unsuccessfully trying to move them on.

As she caught up, Rose realised Fudge had already texted a photo to Sharon.

'Shazza says it's definitely an escape pod,' Fudge told Rose. 'Look.'

Sure enough, about four hundred metres away, the subject of everyone's attention was a cobalt-blue metal globe, nearly two metres across, embedded in a massive crater. A hatchway in the side was wide open, and a sickly yellow light was pulsating outwards, flickering through some smoke emerging from inside as well.

Instinctively protective, Rose pulled Fudge behind her, in case the yellow glow was dangerous. But Fudge was too excited to care about things like safety. He took a photo of the hatchway, then showed it to her, pinching the photo to zoom in on the interior of the globe.

'Oh my god, Rose,' he squeaked. 'It's empty. That means it got out – there's an alien on the loose!'

Rose was about to say something comforting, trying

to assure him everything was okay, but she didn't need to. Fudge wasn't alarmed at all.

'It's so exciting!' he yelled and ran back down the alleyway, probably to have a quick chat with Sharon. Those two …

Then it occurred to Rose that maybe she could get some photos. *That* would prove to Gran that the spaceship stuff was all real.

She headed back down the alleyway to get her phone.

And then she froze.

The wheelie bins out the back of number 27? Did they just … move?

Rose frowned. Trick of the light? No, that recycling bin had definitely shifted sideways.

Could be a dog. Or another animal?

'You okay?' she said quietly, not wanting to scare whoever or whatever it was. Carefully she eased the bins apart and saw what had hidden there.

It wasn't a dog. Or a cat. Or a fox. Or anything on Earth.

The thing was white; a ball of soft furry whiteness, just under a metre wide. It was standing there, upright on two little pink clawed feet, no visible legs. It had furry arms that might've been lost against the white fur of the body if it hadn't been for the cute pink paws with tiny suckers on the ends of its long, spindly fingertips. It had big pink ears, a bit like a rabbit's, flattened to its head as if it were more afraid of her than she was of it.

But it was the face of the thing that amazed Rose the most. Soulful was the only word Rose could think of. Huge almond eyes, watery as if they were about to shed tears, blinked at her. There was a teeny-tiny snout and beneath that a sad little mouth.

Instead of being scared, Rose felt an overwhelming desire to reach out and hug the creature. It was the cutest thing she had ever seen. She put her hand to her mouth, breathing slowly before muttering to herself, 'Oh my god, what are you?'

The one thing Rose had not expected was a reply.

'*Meep meep,*' the adorable beastie said, a slight tremor in their curious, high-pitched voice.

'Wow,' Rose said. 'I mean hello. What are you?'

'I am the Meep.' The creature's ears flapped out so they were now almost horizontal.

'Oh my god, you can talk. In English. Hello! I'm Rose. I'm a … a human. What happened to you?' She glanced up the alleyway, back to the flatwood but no one was coming this way, thankfully. She thought about the escape-pod-thing that had so excited Fudge just now. 'Did you crash?'

The Meep looked up with eyes growing rounder and sadder. 'I fell from the stars,' they said, and held out their right arm. 'I hurt my paw!' the Meep added in utter despair.

Rose took the little offered paw and could see greeny-blue blood oozing from a small cut, almost the same colour as the pod back up at the end of the alleyway.

'Let me see what I can do,' she said, but the Meep whipped the paw back suddenly. Somehow their eyes got even wider, this time in fear, Rose felt sure.

'It's not safe,' the Meep said. 'There are others, from the sky. They are hunting me. To kill me.'

'Who are they?' asked Rose.

The Meep's eyes flicked from side to side, as if the furry little alien expected an attack from all sides at that very moment. They leaned slightly forward towards Rose.

'Monsters!'

UNIFIED INTELLIGENCE TASKFORCE

MEMORANDUM

From: Scientific Adviser's Office
REF: GH1/3691/3202/KSS/mt
British Branch, UNIT

To: All scientific staff

Subject:
APPOINTMENT OF A NEW UK SCIENTIFIC ADVISER.
DESIGNATION: TRAP 2

I am delighted to inform you all that we have a new civilian scientific adviser joining Dr Taylor's team this month. Shirley Anne Bingham comes from a distinguished background in neurosurgery and the latest MOMS trials in Nashville, USA and her home city of Manchester here in Britain. She has also conducted personal research into folate fortification to further the study of spina bifida.

Recently Shirley has been using her skills and theories to test the PNS of a number of alien species that have passed through our hands here at UNIT and has agreed to join us on a full-time basis to continue her research.

I am assigning her to support Colonel Chan's field team in the South East region of the UK for the next two months.

I am sure we will all benefit greatly from Shirley joining us here at UNIT.

Kate S Stewart
Chief Scientific Officer

Malcolm Taylor
Senior Scientific Adviser

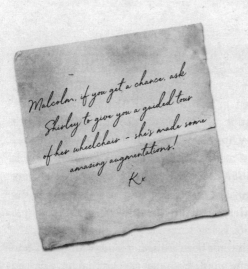

Malcolm, if you get a chance, ask Shirley to give you a guided tour of her wheelchair – she's made some amazing augmentations!

K x

3

The Psychedelic Sun

The Doctor was crouched down behind a UNIT jeep, checking his new jacket pockets to see if his old UNIT pass had transferred over like the psychic paper had. Nope, of course not. Typical. Maybe the psychic paper would suffice if he got caught.

Best thing to do, Doctor, he thought, *is not get caught.*

That cleaner man, Stewart Ferguson, had told him everything he'd witnessed earlier, so it seemed to make sense to the Doctor that the central blast furnace was the place to get to, especially as that was where the spaceship had touched down.

Of course, everyone from UNIT was heading there too.

He looked up. Hovering above the steelworks was a UNIT helicopter, its halogen searchlight scouring the area. Around him were visored troops and a few UNIT people in hazmat suits, being sprayed down with fire-retardant chemicals. A number of civilians, the nightshifters Stew had called them, were being escorted into ambulances by UNIT paramedics and, before long, the ambulances were zooming off.

The Doctor slipped along the wall until he found a locked rusty door. He sonicked it, and the door helpfully clicked open.

Pushing through, the Doctor found himself in the central courtyard area. To the right, higher up, he could see the office complex. Directly ahead was the entrance to the blast furnace area. He reckoned the best way to get into that unseen was from above, rather than ground level, so he slipped up a metal ladder onto a walkway, then up a further one which, as he scurried along it, took him to the same vantage point over the blast furnace area that Stew had been at earlier.

Molten metal was still dripping from a damaged vat, and the UNIT forces were working to seal it. But most importantly, at the heart of the area was the spaceship.

'Beautiful,' the Doctor breathed. 'Awww, that's really classy.'

Sleek, cobalt blue, at the centre of its body was what almost looked like a folded over metal apron, riveted to the body. A second one was present, just above the three massive legs at the base, which were keeping the craft firmly locked into the ground. Back at the top, just below the perfect pointed nozzle, were three red discs, probably sensors of some kind.

More of the hazmat team were spraying at the legs, probably with some coolant, although the Doctor reckoned it wasn't necessary. Any spaceship that could come through a warp field and 'crash' towards the ground but then right itself before landing in a steelworks was probably pretty good at dealing with heat.

The Doctor could see the exposed gash along the side and noted Stew was correct: something had come out rather than gone into the ship. Probably an emergency escape pod leaving at a more acute angle than it had been designed for. He wondered where that had ended up.

Then some voices drifted up from below.

'Make way for Trap Two,' said a male voice with a natural authority to it.

He looked down at a UNIT colonel and a young woman in a wheelchair, making her way around the rubble as if she navigated such things every day.

'Now, I think we're making a fundamental mistake, Colonel.'

'Why so?' he asked her.

She pointed at the spaceship. 'Cos maybe that thing was on a collision course to start with, but look at it.' She held up a tablet; the Doctor couldn't see clearly from this height, but guessed it was showing footage of the craft's descent. 'The spaceship was flying down like this, but then, look, it swings around at about forty-five degrees and then even further and further until, at the last minute, it pulls one hundred and eighty degrees upright and settles down in here, just as we can see it now.'

'So?'

The woman sighed and tapped again at the tablet. 'What I'm saying is, the ship didn't crash. It parked.'

The colonel registered this new fact. 'I see.' He reached over and tapped the tablet himself. 'No signs of life?'

'Not yet,' the woman agreed, giving the spaceship a

onceover. 'But then, we don't know what kind of life we're looking for.'

The colonel looked around. 'You okay here for a moment?'

The woman sighed. 'Of course I am.'

With a nod, the colonel wandered off to talk to his UNIT people.

Keeping an eye on the woman, who was apparently engrossed with her tablet, the Doctor silently shimmied down the metal ladders until he was at ground level, then snuck round to the base of the rocket, between the legs. As he suspected, it wasn't hot. Not a metal he recognised but, despite the simplicity of the ship's design, he guessed it was a lot more sophisticated and advanced than the outward appearance might suggest.

He used his sonic to once again create one of his little floating screens and, second by second, different parts of the ship popped up as he pointed at them with his sonic, giving him both an external view and then a sort of cutaway, showing specs, technical breakdowns, propulsion units …

'Too good for us now?' said a female voice from behind him.

'Evening,' the Doctor said without looking up. 'You know what this is?' he indicated the schematics on his screen.

'No, Doctor,' she said. 'Tell me.'

The Doctor liked her. She wasn't easily fazed, this one. Good. 'That's a Double Bladed Dagger Drive. It's been damaged by laser fire. You know what that means?'

'We've got two sets of visitors, then.'

The Doctor agreed, turning round and shutting down his screen. 'Yup, at war with each other.' He held out a hand and she shook it. The woman was a dark blonde, wearing a pale grey suit over an orange blouse, and had a wide smile that could light up the skies. 'Nice to meet you,' he continued. 'Oh, did you get the heat readings on deceleration?'

The woman in the wheelchair nodded. 'I got everything.' She passed him her tablet and he scanned everything quickly. 'I'm Shirley Anne Bingham, by the way. Mrs. Not a doctor, or a professor. But I am UNIT Scientific Adviser number fifty-six.'

The Doctor grinned at her. 'I was number one.'

'I know,' Shirley said. 'I read the files. I'm gonna get a bonus just for meeting you.' She looked around, checking the colonel and his troops weren't in earshot. 'So, why are you hiding away? We are on the same side.'

'I just …' And he stopped, realising he wasn't quite sure why he was being so cloak and dagger about it all. This was UNIT, after all. Kate Stewart. Jo Grant. Geneva. Sergeant Benton's beef tea. All good things. Shirley was a scientific adviser. These were, more often than not, his friends, even if he didn't approve of the military side of UNIT's 'shoot first ask questions later' processes. So why did he feel so … off about everything?

'It's all a bit mad, Shirley. You see, I don't know who I am any longer.'

'You look like the Doctor to me,' Shirley replied.

'Well, exactly,' the Doctor said. 'The one in the skinny

suit. After that I wear a bow tie. Then I'm a Scotsman. After that, I'm a woman …'

Shirley frowned. 'But that's your future. You can't know that. It's, well, it's forbidden. Isn't it?'

'I regenerated. And she became, well, me. Again.'

'You got your old face back? Why?'

The Doctor shrugged. 'That's what I'm worried about. Because I've got this friend called Donna Noble. And she was my best mate in the whole wide universe. I absolutely love her.'

Shirley's eyebrows rose. So did the Doctor's.

'Oh,' he carried on. 'Do I say things like that now? Is that who I am?' He tried the words out again. 'I love her.'

Shirley smiled. 'Sounds like a nice thing to say.'

The Doctor wanted to agree, but he needed her to realise it wasn't that simple. 'Donna took the mind of a Time Lord into her head. Mine. Sort of mine. Well, a cheap copy of mine, really, but with all the same information, secrets, power. So I had to wipe her memory to save her life. If she ever remembers me, she will die. So off she goes, living her amazing, wonderful life with a husband and a daughter and some Googly Eyes apparently and …'

'You're rambling,' Shirley prodded.

'So what happens next? I get this face back. And guess what, the TARDIS lands right beside her. And then a spaceship crashes right in front of her. Like she's drawing me in.'

Shirley frowned. 'You think she made all this happen?' She indicated the wrecked steelworks and the spaceship.

The Doctor shook his head. 'Oh no, no. She's got no idea. She's so ordinary, and brilliant and with her family, she's so happy now. But now the universe is turning around her again and I don't believe in destiny, Shirley, I really don't, but if destiny does exist, then it's heading for Donna Noble right now.'

Shirley thought on this for a moment. 'Simple question, Doctor. Why?'

'I don't know.' The Doctor started to pace in a circle. 'But Donna can't remember. She mustn't remember, and I won't be the one who kills her.' He let out a long sigh and then stopped wandering and looked at Shirley's tablet again. He smiled at her. 'Right, so that's not an automatic drive, but there's no sign of a pilot. So if they abandoned ship, which that large hole up there suggests, then we should look for some kind of—'

A crisp female voice rang out. 'Ma'am, we've found the escape pod!'

The Doctor dropped expertly into the shadows so no one could see him, as a UNIT sergeant marched round from behind a wall. 'No sign of life,' she reported, 'but we're moving to secure the site.'

'Good work, Sergeant Vaughan. Go get it.'

Sergeant Vaughan went off, and Shirley swivelled her chair round to follow, pausing beside the Doctor. 'And we don't need you, mate, so off you pop. I've got this. Bye-bye.'

The Doctor leaned in close to her ear, and grasped her shoulder admiringly. 'You waited your whole life to meet me, yeah?'

Shirley blew air out of her cheeks. 'You wish,' but winked at him.

The Doctor stepped away as she headed off, confidently navigating the smashed debris on the ground. He'd get to the escape pod site, of course, but on his own terms. He weaved in and out of the wrecked steelworks, until he was close to a group of parked Land Rovers. One of them was full of munitions, meaning no one was likely to get into the back of it.

He saw Sergeant Vaughan walking towards the vehicles so he hopped in and pulled the canvas down, shielding him from her view. He peeked out – oh, and there was Shirley Anne Bingham now with the sergeant.

She saw him. Made eye contact. Winked again.

And then the colonel with whom she'd entered the blast furnace area turned up.

'Colonel Chan.' The sergeant saluted and snapped to attention.

The colonel nodded to Shirley and she relaxed. Chan showed her a small handheld device and she read something on it. 'We think we've got something,' he was explaining. 'A signal. From inside the ship.'

'Back we go,' Shirley said, as the Land Rover the Doctor was hiding in started up its engine.

The Doctor was off to wherever the escape pod had landed. But he did wonder what signal Colonel Chan had been talking about.

At the bottom of the alleyway behind Rose's house, just before it emerged at the corner of Bachelor Road and Hale

Avenue, was a high brick wall that sheltered the garden of this last house. Built into the wall was a tall wooden gate, leading into the garden that allowed old Mrs Higgins who lived there – small, grey-haired, bespectacled, usually wearing a flowery pinny – access to the alleyway.

Fudge knew Mrs Higgins well and frequently helped her put her bins out on the street when it was collection day, in exchange for 50p. Fifty pence didn't really go very far these days, but Mrs Higgins clearly thought it was a fortune to a 10-year-old like Fudge. He had no desire to offend her, so he took it each week and made out it would help towards his saving for a DS-E controller for his PS5. As she had no idea any of those words meant, both were content with this weekly arrangement.

Tomorrow was collection day and, despite all the excitement, Fudge felt it was his duty to once again get Mrs Higgins's bins ready. As he walked towards the gate, he was talking to Shazza Allen on his phone, breathlessly telling her what she had missed by not abandoning her dinner, and simultaneously describing in detail the escape pod which he'd already sent her a photo of and could plainly see for herself.

But that was his and Shazza's friendship all over – text, send a photo, then call to talk over the evidence in detail. 'Yeah, there are aliens on the loose, right on our doorstep, and—'

Fudge stopped talking.

As he flicked up the latch on Mrs Higgins's wooden gate and opened it, Fudge realised he wasn't looking at Mrs Higgins at all.

What he was looking at was tall.

Very, very tall.

And not wearing glasses or a pinny.

It resembled a giant green ant. No, not an ant, a giant green beetle. Well, not really a beetle, more an …

Fudge's brain finally gave up and accepted the truth of it: he was looking at an alien.

He took in the chitinous exoskeleton that encased its wiry body. Two massively muscular legs, bent slightly backwards at the knee like a grasshopper. Two arms – one thin, with a six-fingered hand at the end holding a ray gun straight out of *Dark Descent*. The left arm however was chunky and looked like it had been lifting weights for ten years solid, and in place of a hand was a huge claw with serrated edges, which opened and closed in time with Fudge's panicked breathing. The head was expressionless, dominated by two massive red pupilless eyes, each the size of a car headlight, and below them, a small thin mouth. Atop the head, two small twitching antennae.

Fudge couldn't say a word. He had heard his mum use the expression 'My heart was in my mouth' once with no idea what it really meant. Right now, though, he understood. Really, really clearly.

The alien looked down, red eyes blazing brighter as it regarded him.

'Fudge? You there, mate?'

Fudge could hear Shazza's voice on the phone, but he couldn't reply.

The alien's mouth opened rounder, bigger, but not wider. A tongue snaked out and, like the antennae, it seemed to be searching for something. It came further and further towards Fudge's face, which should have been impossible (where was it coming from, the creature's stomach?) and yet it was happening.

Fudge saw long tendrils, like fingers, emerge from both the tip and sides of the tongue. They whipped forward and grabbed his chin.

Fudge screamed. He'd never screamed in his life until now. But the bug-alien, with fingers on its tongue, was enough to break the habit of a lifetime.

The tongue-fingers immediately let go of him and the whole tongue whipped back inside the mouth.

Fudge ran for his life.

Had he stayed another second, he would have seen a second bug-alien emerge from Mrs Higgins's garden, and stop the first one giving chase.

'Leave him,' the new bug-alien said. 'It's the Meep we seek. Continue the hunt.'

The two bug-aliens started marching back up the alleyway, unaware that they were heading straight towards their prey.

Back at the Millson Wagner Steelworks, Colonel Chan and Shirley Anne Bingham were making their way through the rubble towards the blast furnace chamber and the spaceship.

Chan was still using his handheld device to monitor the signal they had picked up. He passed it to Shirley, who stopped her wheelchair and examined the signal.

'It's some kind of repeated pulse,' Chan said.

'Have you tried replying?' asked Shirley.

Chan nodded, taking the device back, and they moved on and came to the entrance to the blast furnace chamber.

'When we answered,' Chan explained, 'we used a basic modulation and it modulated straight back but—'

He stopped, as did Shirley.

Around the spaceship, the UNIT team had constructed a scaffold, reaching up to an unopened doorway about a third of the way up, lower down and on the opposite side to the gash through which the escape pod had left.

Shirley looked at the steps up to the scaffolding, then at her chair and finally offered Chan a raised eyebrow.

Chan sighed and closed his eyes in a mixture of frustration at his team and his own embarrassment that he hadn't thought of access for her either.

'I'm really sorry,' he began. 'You see, Geneva said to go in immediately and—'

Shirley waved it aside. 'Don't make me the problem, just get in there.'

Colonel Chan smiled at her. 'Yes, ma'am.'

'And Colonel? Be careful.'

Chan started the climb up and eventually joined Sergeant Vaughan and four privates who were already waiting outside the door.

Shirley strained to try and see what they were doing, but in her current position and angle, everything was obscured by the scaffolding, so she wheeled herself back a bit. Now she could see.

The doorway was flush to the ship's side, indented slightly. It was more of an outline than an actual physical door.

She could hear Vaughan barking orders to one of her men. 'Okay, let's see if this key-pulse works, thank you. Jackson?'

A soldier saluted her and Chan pressed a small white box against the door-outline. It began bleeping and a circle of red lights flickered on and off.

'At arms,' commanded Chan and all the soldiers readied their guns. 'Do not fire,' he added. 'Not without my command.'

Shirley could see them tighten their grips on their weapons. Unconsciously, she did the same to the wheels on her chair.

Beep beep beep.

She realised she was holding her breath, so she let it out.

PING!

She could see that the red lights had gone green.

As the door slid upwards, Shirley couldn't really see whatever the UNIT soldiers could see. Damn, she needed to get further around and—

Light! A swirling pulsating rhythmic light. She strained her eyes, trying to see through it and could just about make out possibly a globe, or an orb of some sort, floating in mid-air. It was impossible to be sure from down where she was, but the light certainly seemed to be emanating from it.

And from within it there seemed to be a loud ... well, wailing. Like a thousand cries all at once.

Then the light changed, it seemed to be more than just light. It had a pattern to it, no, more embedded within it.

Shirley thought it was vaguely psychedelic, like she used to see on posters from the 1960s.

The screaming sound stopped suddenly. That was weird.

She was going to shout up to Chan and his soldiers when she heard a series of clangs as each soldier simply dropped their gun. Some landed on the scaffold next to them; a couple fell all the way down to the ground near her.

The tendrils of light, as far as Shirley could see, were flowing into the UNIT troops, through their ears, through their eyes, through their mouths perhaps?

Then the light stopped. Switched off.

And the door slid shut again, cutting off the orb from the soldiers' view and Shirley's.

She was about to move forward, to greet Chan and the soldiers who were starting to clamber back down the scaffolding, but some sixth sense told her – no.

Instead she rolled back, further into the shadows, melting into the darkness as the Doctor had before her.

As the soldiers walked past, Shirley had to stop herself gasping out loud.

It was clear to see that each of them, including Sergeant Vaughan and Colonel Chan, no longer had normal eyes. The pupils, the whites, everything had been replaced by the same swirling psychedelic patterns of light she'd seen come out of the orb just now.

One by one, they lowered their helmet visors, meaning no one would know they'd been affected. Altered.

And then they were gone, out of the chamber and presumably heading outside towards the parked vehicles.

Horrified, Shirley Anne Bingham stayed exactly where she was and started formulating a plan of what to do next.

Hidden in the back of the moving Land Rover, the Doctor was gritting his teeth. The boxes of munitions weren't exactly designed for lying on, all hard lines and pointy edges – and the driver didn't seem to grasp that speed bumps in the road were designed to keep traffic at the regulation 20mph and not close to 40.

Finally the transport stopped and the Doctor prepared himself to make any explanation he could think of if someone came round the back, opened up the flap and found him.

After 30 seconds, no one did.

After another 10 seconds, he eased himself over the boxes and then opened the flap himself, realised no one was watching and slipped out.

About six military vehicles were parked there, blocking the street, stopping anyone getting in or out.

A street sign told him he was on Hale Avenue, and just off it was Bachelor Road and – oh, look! There was a convenient little alleyway he could slip into and… whoops, no, not yet. Because whatever the UNIT troops were after seemed to be up that same alleyway. And they were marching along it now.

'All troops to the flatwood area,' one of them was barking into a radio. 'Surround the pod, surround and secure!'

The Doctor opted to wait a minute longer and see what happened.

Leila.krishnam@senenet.co.ae

18 November

To: Rose Noble

Re: Latest shipment

Hey lovely Rose

Just wanted to say the latest shipment of your toys has safely arrived in Abu Dhabi. Thank you for packing them so well.

I'll let you know how soon I need another shipment, though probably not until early in the New Year. Everyone here absolutely loves them, especially my friends in Fujairah and Dubai. Even my dad says to tell you that, and I quote, 'Rose has an amazing, imaginative product that is unique.' See, told you! Your designs are going down a treat and everyone is talking about them.

Happy Christmas to you and your mum

Leila x

4

Hour of the Beast

Stew Ferguson was feeling... tense might not have been the right word, but unrelaxed would certainly do.

He'd done as that Doctor bloke had told him: count to 100 then make a dash for it, back out beyond the steelworks and into north London. And keep going till he got home.

All good advice except that Stew had counted to 100 at least five times now, each time getting to 98 ... 99 ... and then deciding there were still too many people around.

He'd watched trucks and Land Rovers come and go, he'd seen weird lights from inside the steelworks. He'd heard noises and he'd seen people in visors immediately outside.

He couldn't help but hope the Doctor would come back and get him. There again, maybe the Doctor had himself been 'got' by the army guys.

Deep breath, Stew, he thought. *Then run. Get home. Call Billy. Tell him everything.*

Stew Ferguson finally stood up, collected himself, prepared to run. He yanked open the door – and found himself facing a visored UNIT soldier.

'Hello,' he managed.

The soldier raised his visor and for a second Stew thought the poor guy had had an accident inside the smelting plant. His eyes were all burned and...

No. They weren't burned. They were glowing with psychedelic patterns.

Then Stewart Ferguson suddenly stopped seeing anything except the glowing. And began hearing a voice in his head, telling him what to do next.

It didn't involve running home...

Sylvia Noble was feeling a little less tense.

Donna was focusing on her job-hunting and thankfully no longer talking about spaceships as Rose came thundering down the stairs, through the hall, past Sylvia and Donna in the kitchen without saying a word. Somehow she manged to slow down just enough to open the back door rather than crash through it.

Donna rather pointlessly called out, 'It's bin night, and it's your turn...' but if Rose even heard her, it didn't matter. She was already running down to her shed.

'Wonder what she wanted her school bag for?' Sylvia said.

'What bag?' Donna asked.

Sylvia sighed. 'You really don't see anything, do you? And then quickly added 'Which is a good thing. Usually. I mean—'

But Donna was already closing her laptop and getting ready to go after Rose, pulling a THINGS TO DO list off the corkboard beside her.

* * *

Rose crashed through the door of the shed somehow out of breath just from running a few metres. Must be the excitement, she thought. She stopped, looking around the tiny shed, trying to work out where her new friend had gone.

There they were, near the back, frozen in fear, probably at the noise and wind that had heralded Rose's arrival, or the swinging of the coloured lights hanging from the ceiling.

'Sorry,' Rose said. 'It's only me.' She held up the schoolbag. 'I got some first aid stuff.'

The Meep pointed around the room at all of the stuffed toys that Rose had been creating and selling around the world. 'I made some little friends,' they said with a certain amount of childlike pride.

'They're just toys,' Rose explained. But the Meep wasn't listening. Or understanding, more like.

The Meep picked up one of the toys. 'Please be my friend,' they said. Their wide eyes saddened and their little mouth downturned further as the toy, unsurprisingly as far as Rose was concerned, said absolutely nothing.

'Why won't you speak to the little Meep?' the Meep pleaded. Then with a sudden burst of frustration, the Meep chucked the toy into a corner and picked up another, different one. 'Be my friend?' No reply. Wham, it went into a different corner. Another toy. 'Be my friend?' Nothing. Another corner gained a new soft toy at some velocity.

Toy after toy, the same question, the same lack of answer, the same hurling away. Rose managed to catch one of the toys as it was thrown, then another. 'No, no,' she explained. 'They can't talk.'

The Meep stared at the toy they were currently holding and then, somewhat over-demonstratively, hugged it close to their own furry white body. 'Poor little things with no voice!'

And Rose caught the Meep's sad look and again felt an overwhelming desire to just hug them for hours and hours and ...

Rose took a breath. 'Look, it's just my little homemade business.' She sat on a chair by a sewing machine and held up the bag of Googly Eyes and some of the furs she and her mum had bought home from Camden earlier. She indicated a spreadsheet pinned to the wall of orders and a few emails from her customers tacked to a cork board. 'I'm trying to make a bit of money for Mum and Dad, that's all. Cos they need it.' Rose pointed to some of them, naming them, and the Meep looked at each one in turn, not understanding any of it. Best-Puplet. King-Rhino. Blobby McBlobbyface. She then held the little toy up that she'd caught. 'I call this one Captain Potato. They're all toys. Humans have toys.' She turned Captain Potato over and tugged at an almost invisible zip sewn into his back and began pulling out his stuffing. 'You see, toys have stuffing inside—'

And the Meep let out an extraordinarily high-pitched and noisy screech of pure terror. 'You pulled its tummy out!' they shrieked. And then continued screaming.

Very, very loudly.

Rose desperately begged the Meep to be quiet. 'Keep it down,' she pleaded. 'Don't be so loud.' But the Meep was running around in circles, grabbing more toys, checking

Rose hadn't ripped their tummies out too, while still shrieking and screaming, ears flapping, eyes widening.

'Oh my god,' yelled Rose, almost as loudly. 'How did you ever manage to fly a spaceship?'

It was like a switch had been flicked. At the sound of 'spaceship', the Meep just stopped dead still, all panic about the toys forgotten, it seemed, and a sad look settled on their face. 'I need my ship. I want to go home.' And then, wringing their tiny paws, ears flat, eyes bigger than ever, they looked at Rose. 'The Meep is all alone.'

Rose dropped to the ground beside the Meep and took the paws in her own hands. 'I know that feeling. Sometimes I think I'm from a different planet.' She smiled at the Meep, who seemed to smile in return. Just a little closed-mouth smile of solidarity. 'Or that's what other people say.'

The Meep stroked Rose's cheek. 'You sound lonely.'

Rose gave a half-smile. 'No, just ... different.'

'Now you have the Meep.'

'Yeah,' Rose agreed. 'Maybe we can help each other.' She so wanted to reach out, give the Meep a huge hug.

'I'd like that,' the Meep said in the sweetest voice Rose had ever heard.

Rose went in for the hug – and suddenly she heard her mum right outside the shed.

'I told you,' Mum was saying. Well, almost yelling, really. Mum's voice tended to shift between a whisper and a yell without much in between. 'It's on the rota. It's your turn, Rose, but do you listen? Do you even look at the rota?'

'Hide,' Rose hissed at the Meep, and leapt up to intercept what she knew was coming next.

Sure enough, the shed door was yanked open and Mum was standing there, binbag in hand. 'Every week, it's the same thing,' she said. She held the bag out for Rose to take. 'Who ends up doing the bins?' She pointed at her own chest. 'Me!'

'Mum,' Rose yelled, more aggressively than she intended. She moved to block the doorway and pointed towards the KEEP OUT sign on the outside wall. 'Mum, what does it say?'

But her mum was having none of it. 'You know my rules. No secrets in this house.' She looked around the shed. 'You got anything for recycling?'

'I've already done it, Mum,' Rose said, doing everything except physically shoving her mum back out, trying to look round unsuspiciously, to see where the Meep had gone. 'No, look, I'm starving. Let's go and have some of Gran's curry, yeah?'

Too late. Her mum had seen the Meep. Standing at the back, frozen, not moving. Not even breathing. A giant fluffy white toy amidst all the smaller ones.

She stepped closer to it. 'That one's new, isn't it?' Donna bent over, stroking the white fur. 'Oh, that's your best yet.'

'Yeah, I know,' Rose said, trying to ease her mum away from 'the best yet' as fast as possible.

'That woman in Abu Dhabi who buys your stuff, she'll love that one.' Mum straightened up. That was a start, Rose thought. But no, her mum carried on. 'She's obsessed with gonks and stuff. What's her name? Leila or something? A grown woman obsessed with … dollies.' She pointed at the Meep. 'You should charge her double for that one.'

Rose nodded. 'Yeah, right. Now look, it's really cold.' She faked a shiver for dramatic effect. 'Shall we go in?

But Mum was staring at the Meep again. 'I've got to say, that's very good handiwork. You could go on the Sewing Bee.' She peered closer. 'And those eyes are amazing. They look so real.'

Rose held her breath. Gazing in wonder, her mum was breathing right on the Meep's face now.

And the Meep blinked.

Mum jumped back and pointed at the Meep. 'What?'

'What?' Rose asked innocently.

'Did it just …?' and Mum poked the Meep in the right eye.

At which point the Meep screamed in shock and pain.

And Mum stared as the Meep suddenly started running around, one paw over their pained eye.

'What the actual hell?'

She pushed past Rose and flung open the shed door. 'Get out of my garden! You monster!'

At that moment, in the back of the Land Rover parked in Hale Avenue, the Doctor made a decision.

He'd need to get into one of the houses on Bachelor Road, which no doubt would involve vaulting over a series of garden fences in parallel with the alleyway, without being seen, and then—

All his plans changed when he heard a yell.

A bellow, really.

'Get out of my garden!' came the shouting, followed by an even angrier, 'You monster!'

Normally he would have assumed a UNIT soldier had been spotted and some neighbour was being stroppy.

But no, that voice belonged to Donna Noble. Which meant, bearing in mind a lifetime of coincidence, patterns and universal destinies he didn't believe in, she had actually found a real life, honest-to-goodness monster in her garden.

And she did not sound happy about it ...

Rose was starting to panic. No, no, that was wrong, she was already panicking. The Meep, instead of fleeing into the alleyway as her mum had demanded, ran instead into the centre of the garden and then up the path towards the back door, which was flung open by Gran, who clearly wanted to know what all the commotion was about.

At which point the Nobles' garden became, well, very very loud. With lots of shouting, simultaneously.

Rose was quietest, and she was frantically yelling, 'Mum, I promise you, it's okay, just calm down, don't scare it!'

The Meep was shrieking still, half-blindly crashing into the fence and then into Mum's legs, crying out, 'Pretty, pretty lady, please like the Meep. I'm sorry!'

Mum was yelling louder than Rose and the Meep put together, which was some feat. 'It talks? How the hell does it talk?'

But beneath all of that, Rose realised the strangest reaction was from her gran, who wasn't really looking at the Meep at all, but at Mum.

'Donna,' she was saying. 'Don't look at it, look away. Right now!' And weirdest of all, in utter contradiction of the evidence, Gran added, 'It's not real.'

Sylvia had no doubt that the little white chubby rabbit/cat/thing was an alien. She took that for granted. But all she could focus on was Donna. Her daughter. Her daughter who, if she learned of aliens and spaceships and time travel and tall thin men in suits in police boxes again, would die as her brain burned up.

She was about to go out and physically drag her daughter away from the alien when there was a loud hammering on the door.

And a voice yelling, 'Let me in! Let! Me! In!'

That didn't sound like Shaun. Besides, he had a key and—

Hang on; she realised she knew that voice.

Fifteen years of fear and resentment and a real need to wallop something came out in one hissed, acidic word. 'You!'

She ran up the hallway to the front door as the letterbox was poked open and bent down to see a pair of familiar eyes looking through.

'Hello, Sylvia, nice to see you again. Could you let me in?'

And, quieter and more restrained than she'd ever thought she would manage in all the scenarios she'd pictured in her head of this moment, she bent in closer and spoke to him. 'You said if she sees you again, she will die!'

The Doctor's eyes wrinkled as he was probably giving a mental shrug. 'Well, no actually. If she remembers me is what I said. And that's slightly different.'

Behind them, Donna and Rose were in the kitchen. Donna was furious. Not with Rose. Or the white fluffy thing, but with her. With Sylvia.

'No such things as spaceships? We've got a bloody Martian in the shed!'

Rose was trying to calm her down. 'Stop panicking, Mum, and grow up!'

'Get away from here now,' Sylvia hissed through the letterbox. She then turned back to give Donna another concerned look.

The alien was hanging on to her leg now, like a baby.

Donna shook her leg. 'Get off me, space rat!'

'Help me, pretty lady,' the alien was screeching. 'Help the Meep!'

'Awwww, he's so cute,' said the Doctor. Then his face vanished and the letter box snapped shut.

Sylvia was moving towards Donna. 'Don't look at it, Donna, don't look, don't look. It's not real!'

She dimly heard a strange whirring sound. Suddenly the front door opened behind her just as she reached the kitchen. Donna was still trying to shake the alien off her leg; Rose was nearly beside herself in frustration.

The Doctor walked up to them all.

And Sylvia slapped him round the face.

So hard. So very hard. Nowhere near as hard as she'd always imagined she would slap him, but still, it was immensely satisfying.

'Here we go again,' he said, rubbing his cheek.

Rose was staring at him. 'It's that man.'

Sylvia was horrified. They'd seen him before?

'It's the skinny man from Camden,' Donna said.

'No it isn't!' Sylvia placed herself between the Doctor and her family, holding her arms out as if that might stop him being visible. She was giving Donna a fixed stare. 'He's not there. You can't see him. There's no monster on your leg either. None of this is happening, none of it. For the love of god, none of this is real!'

And everything went silent. Donna's eyes were looking beyond Sylvia. So was Rose. Even the alien thing was staring too. Sylvia's own head turned in time with the Doctor's.

Standing in the hallway, smiling at the insanity he'd just walked in on, was Shaun Temple.

'Eh-eh, Dad's home.'

No one said anything.

It was clear that Shaun could see the Doctor. And Rose. And Donna. And Sylvia. And most importantly of all, the white furry alien holding on to his wife's leg.

He looked at each one in turn before finally settling on Sylvia. 'Something smells nice,' he said, nodding his head towards the cooktop.

'Tuna madras,' Sylvia managed to squeak.

The Meep let go of Donna's legs and looked at them all with huge almond eyes.

'Meep, meep,' it said.

Sylvia felt an inexplicable desire to hug it; a feeling outweighed by longing for the earth to open up and swallow them all.

Up on the flatwood, Colonel Chan was standing close to the abandoned escape pod. Sergeant Vaughan was bent in front of it, peering inside.

Chan surveyed the scrubland. Private Jackson and the rest of his troops were moving the curious civilians further back. Like Chan, their helmet-visors still covered their eyes.

Three UNIT soldiers emerged from further away, the ones Chan had sent out earlier. He looked at the leader. Young. Tall. Sikh, black turban, immaculate uniform, earpiece in place so he could hear all the UNIT chatter.

Why couldn't Chan recall his name?

Whatever was inside his head accessed his memories and suddenly, it came back: *Shervan Singh. Major. Recently transferred down from Chester.*

'Major Singh,' Chan said, 'you and your squad will return to the steelworks immediately.'

Singh frowned and held up a tablet. 'But sir, we've detected an atypical thermal signature at grid five-five-seven and—'

Chan ignored him. 'You will return immediately. For reassignment. Do you understand my order?'

Singh saluted. 'Sir.' He yelled to his two men, 'Mason, Jilvani, we're moving out.'

Chan watched as the three men headed back down the alleyway to wherever their vehicles were parked.

Behind his visor, Chan closed his eyes. In his mind's eye, all he could see was swirling psychedelia. 'We are close,' he breathed. 'The Meep is near.'

As Singh and his two men passed Mrs Higgins's house and went back out into the road, the gate opened and four bug-aliens stepped out.

The one who had tongue-gripped young Fudge earlier showed his commander a readout on his right wrist. 'We have detected a trail. It is Meep blood.'

The commanding bug-alien nodded. 'Then we follow and find the creature.' It regarded its fellows. 'Before it is too late.'

And they started up the alleyway, towards the shed at the back of the garden of number 23.

Inside the living room at the front of number 23, a strange tableau was playing out. Sylvia, Donna, Rose and Shaun, the family, were all standing in silence as the newcomer to the house, the Doctor, jacket chucked over a chair, was casually bandaging up the paw of an alien, the Meep.

It wasn't something that happened very often anywhere but for fifteen years, Sylvia had done her best to make it sure it certainly never happened here.

If only she could explain to Donna, or Rose, or even Shaun why she was so agitated, so hostile towards the Doctor.

Instead, she tugged Donna aside, back towards the hall,

hoping to distract her and move her into the kitchen. 'I'm worried about infection,' she lied. 'From that... beast. I'm sure that man can handle it all. We should leave him alone and, oh, let's go to my house and—'

But Donna was already pulling away from her mum and moving further into the room.

Towards the Doctor.

The Doctor was looking at Donna as she did that familiar old head-wobble-while-barking-at-you thing. Oh, how he'd missed that.

'Never mind the ferret from Mars, who the hell are you?'

The Doctor looked up, clearly unsure how to answer. All he could see and hear in his mind's eye was Donna... breaking. In the TARDIS. Looking so sad as she realised her own fate.

Binary, binary, binary...

'I'm...' he glanced to Sylvia who gave him her best 'don't you dare' look. 'Um...' He turned to Shaun. 'What was it?'

Shaun frowned. 'You said you were a friend of Nerys's.'

The Doctor clicked his fingers. 'That's it,' and beamed at Sylvia as if that explained everything.

Sylvia's frosty look quickly evaporated that smile.

But Donna was getting it. 'Nerys!' she seethed. 'Well now it all makes sense. That viper in the nest!' Sylvia tried to ease Donna away again, but Donna was having none of it. 'I'm not going anywhere, Mum! Look we could sell Mad Paddington here for a million quid!'

Rose was aghast, Shaun appalled. The Doctor turned to reassure the Meep, who had clearly realised that Mad Paddington was aimed in their direction: 'Meep, meep?'

Donna looked at Shaun and Rose. 'Well, you find the money to fill the fridge then!'

Across the road, Fudge Mirchandani was looking through his bedroom window whilst talking to Shazza on the phone. He'd told her about the bug-aliens, and the escape pod and was now relaying that Bachelor Road was swarming with soldiers. Every few moments, a new contingent arrived. This latest lot had helmets with visors down, making them look scarier than all the others.

'This is going to be huge,' he told her and reached forward and opened the window up, so he could lean further out and see more of what was happening.

It was getting busier and busier and noisier and noisier, as troops were making everyone stay in their homes.

Sylvia was pleased to see the Doctor pat the Meep's bandaged paw and the little furry monster settle on the floor. They could both go away now. A long way away.

The Doctor then looked up at Donna. 'What did happen to all your money?'

Typically Donna answered a question with another question. 'Why are you so interested in us? Everywhere we go, there you are.'

Sylvia held her breath, afraid of what the Doctor might say in reply. But a photo seemed to have caught his eye

– a picture of her dad, smiling, in a red bobble hat, up at his allotment.

'I was wondering…' the Doctor went on, staring at the photo. 'There's one person missing. I used to know your granddad, Wilf. Is he…?'

Donna was suddenly quieter. 'No, he's not with us any more.'

The Doctor looked like he'd been hit by a three-tonne weight; all the air seemed to leave him and he sagged down against a chair. 'Right. Of course. He wasn't young…'

Sylvia was astonished. Were those tears welling up in his eyes?

'I loved that man,' the Doctor continued, his voice cracking. 'I'm so sorry for your loss.'

Donna frowned. 'He's not dead!'

'You idiot,' Sylvia added.

'He's in sheltered accommodation,' Donna explained. 'He's ninety-four, and couldn't manage the stairs.'

'We were lucky,' Shaun chipped in. 'We couldn't afford it, then this offer came along.'

Rose enthusiastically nodded along. 'It's amazing, he's got this room, like a cottage, with a garden, and it's almost free.'

'Run by that lot in the middle of London, UNIT,' Shaun said. 'This woman in charge, Kate something, she said he's an old soldier and that she'd take care of him.'

The Doctor got up, beaming brightly. 'Awww, Kate, yeah, I know her. She's looking after Wilf? Brilliant. That's brilliant. Now then, the Meep!' He started to pace around. 'I promise I can help to get him home again,' he told Rose, then turned to Sylvia. 'And then you will never see me again.'

'You're assuming "he" as a pronoun,' said Rose.

'True,' the Doctor admitted. 'Yes, sorry, good point.' He crouched back down to the Meep and Donna automatically sat on the arm of the sofa next to him.

Sylvia held her breath again.

'Are you he, or she,' the Doctor said, 'or they or …?'

The Meep's eyes narrowed fractionally. 'My chosen pronoun is the definite article. I am always the Meep.'

'Oh, I do that too,' the Doctor said with a quick smile round at everyone in the room. 'Now,' he continued to the little alien. 'You were shot down. Why? Who wants you dead?'

'The Wrarth Warriors.' The Meep's eyes started to fill with tears.

Sylvia maternal instincts suddenly kicked in again, and she wanted to hug the poor lost little soul.

'They cultivate Meepkind for our beautiful fur. The galaxy said, "No more fur, it's wrong," but the Wrarth Warriors' reaction to that was to slaughter all their livestock. Now they will hunt me down until there is no more Meepkind left.' The Meep reached out with its wounded paw to touch the back of the Doctor's hand. 'It breaks both my hearts.'

The Doctor grinned and stood up. 'You've got two hearts? So have I!'

'You've got what?' Donna also stood up, dangerously close to him.

79

'No,' Sylvia snapped. 'He means it like a metaphor, like in two minds.' She threw him the filthiest look she could muster. 'Don't you?'

Before the Doctor could respond, there was a massively loud hammering on the front door.

'All right,' Shaun yelled. 'We're coming.'

'Open up,' shouted a voice.

The Doctor was already heading towards the front door, leaving Donna looking at Shaun and Rose. 'What the hell is it now?'

Leaving Donna, Shaun and Rose with the Meep thing, Sylvia went out into the hall with the Doctor, who had slipped his jacket back on.

'It's all good,' the Doctor told her, reaching out to open the door. 'It's the soldiers. We need a lift, so me and the Meep can get out of your way.'

That sounded perfect to Sylvia.

The Doctor pulled open the door, saying, 'This lot are on my side.'

The two soldiers standing in the doorway didn't look friendly. They were clad in black, armed, wearing helmets with visors hiding their faces.

Sylvia felt a chill go down her spine. This felt wrong. Hostile.

'We demand to search the house,' said one of them. 'This has been declared a military zone.'

'Sorry, could you say that again?' the Doctor asked and got that strange metal tool thing out of his pocket. Wilf had once called it a screwdriver of some sort, but it didn't look like a screwdriver to Sylvia.

It whirred, and the visor on the soldier who'd spoken lifted up by itself. Sylvia gasped.

The soldier had no eyes to speak of, just a psychedelic sort of light. A line about kaleidoscope eyes from an old Beatles song went through her head. She drew in a breath.

The Doctor whirred his screwdriver thing and the visor came down again.

The soldier didn't seem to even realise it had happened. 'We demand to search the house,' he repeated as the visor lowered. 'This has been declared a military zone.'

'Not today thank you.' The Doctor closed the door on the two soldiers, then looked back at Sylvia. 'I'm sorry, but I think we need to run.'

Sylvia was about to tell him exactly what he could do with that idea when she felt a wave of heat against her back and heard a colossal explosion.

She swung round, looked down the hall to the kitchen only to see a large part of the rear wall and the back door were no longer there.

Instead, two large bug-like aliens filled the space, aiming blasters at her and the Doctor.

'Surrender the Meep!' one of them shouted in a guttural voice that sounded like it was going down a badly blocked drain.

The Doctor grabbed Sylvia's hand and hauled her back into the living room, ignoring the astonished looks on the faces of the rest of the Noble family.

At which point another huge explosion occurred and Sylvia watched as the front door to number 23 crashed down onto the floor of the hallway.

Immediately this was followed by bullets, presumably fired by the soldiers outside the front door, and blue beams of sizzling light fired by, she supposed, the bug-aliens in the kitchen.

Number 23 Bachelor Road was suddenly the centre of a pitched battle between two different armies, and the house was getting the worst part of the deal.

She looked at the Doctor.

'Sorry,' he mouthed at her.

If she survived this, she'd make him sorry all right...

The Holy Writs and Strictures
of the Shadow Proclamation

Article 29
Convention [301]

Seeking the universal ratification of the Shadow Proclamation, Scholars from Rago Rago 56 Rago have put forward a proposal to genetically engineer a military constabulary to support and enhance the judiciary constabulary already supplied by the Judoon (*see Article 04 Convention* [179]).

It is proposed that the Scholars will distil and then combine traits from five powerful species, mainly taken from the inhabitants of the Wrarth System, to wit: the internal organs of the Birastrop (*see Article 04 Convention* [84]), encased within an insectoid exoskeleton adapted from the Tritovore (*see Article 04 Convention* [200]); the detachable and extendable limbs, wings and mandibles of the Collusc (*see Article 04 Convention* [463]); the highly developed brain of the Sensafillia (*see Article 04 Convention* [811]) operating the eyes and ears of the Uvodni (*see Article 04 Convention* [202]).

Once these traits have been combined, the Scholars theorise the Shadow Proclamation will have access to a fighting force capable of existing on at least Level 5, 6 and 11 worlds as well the ability to operate in the near vacuum of space itself.

It is proposed that a period of 28-apple-point-6 time spans be set aside to observe the ultimate creatures that are bred in the Scholar's vats, provisionally decreed to be Wrarth Warriors, to ensure their loyalty, reliability and intellect meets the highest requirements of the Shadow Proclamation.

__The Shadow Architect's office has approved and witnessed these protocols and progressed them to the Article 29 Shadow Committee for final ratification.__

5
Revenge of the Wrarth

Having already blocked off one end of Bachelor Road, Colonel Chan was now directing his troops to park vehicles across the street just outside number 23, creating a secondary blockade.

'Secure the house,' he said.

With his mission accomplished, the power controlling his mind brought him a feeling of euphoria and self-satisfaction. But it wasn't to last.

He had sent Sergeant Vaughan and two soldiers to the front door, to gain access. But the door had blown open and both soldiers thrown to the ground, hit by blasts of energy that Chan knew weren't human.

Wrarth Warriors. The words appeared unbidden in his mind. Yes, these Wrarth Warriors were the aggressors.

Vaughan fired back into the hallway even while dropping back. Chan opted to join the battle himself. 'Take the house,' he barked at the soldiers. 'Repeat, take the house!' Taking out his pistol, he stepped over the downed troops and into the building's cramped hallway.

Watching this from his window, terrified, was young

Fudge, still tapping furiously on his phone, sending texts and photos to Shazza Allen as fast as he could.

The Noble family, the Doctor and the Meep were cowering in the living room. The hallway was a mess of blasted plaster, wood chips, crumbled brick and broken glass, torn apart by UNIT bullets and Wrarth Warrior energy blasts.

It was noisy, it was relentless and, above all, it was damn scary.

'What the hell is going on?' Donna yelled to everyone and no one in particular.

'There's children in here,' Shaun shouted.

The gunfire rattled on, and Rose looked at her father. 'Never mind me, we've got to save the Meep!'

The Doctor meanwhile was peering up over the top of the radiator just below the front room window, trying to get an idea of what was happening directly outside the front door.

Make this stop! Sylvia wanted to scream at him. *Before Donna is killed. Before we all are.*

The Doctor dropped away from the window. 'When was this terrace built?' he asked quite randomly.

'1910,' Shaun answered automatically.

'And where's your cab?'

'Down the street. Opposite number 15, Billy's place.'

The Doctor looked from left to right. 'Which way is that?'

Shaun pointed to the right.

'My old car's nearer,' Sylvia shouted. 'Blue Kia Picanto. Parked right outside the front door.'

'And hemmed in by UNIT barricades,' the Doctor said. 'But thank you,' he added, with a cheerful smile.

Sylvia didn't smile back.

The Doctor flattened himself against the radiators and got out his screwdriver thing. 'Okay, let me concentrate.'

And then he did something quite extraordinary – something even Sylvia had to admit was impressive. From the end of his screwdriver thing, four smaller prongs had emerged and now all five tips were glowing with a bright white light. And with these five lights, he was now drawing a see-through shape in the air, a rectangle nearly two metres high.

Like a huge TV screen resting on its side.

'I saw him do this before,' she heard Rose whisper.

Sylvia watched anxiously as Donna stared at the screen and the screwdriver. There was wonder on her face, and something more. Recognition?

Oh god, not now, she thought, *please, not now…*

Gradually the rectangle's shimmering orange outline filled in sheet-metal grey, hazing the air. The Doctor behind it seemed more a shadow than a clear image.

He put his sonic screwdriver away and then, like a magician, used his hands to ease the floating rectangle through the air, pushing it towards the door. He paused there, creating another rectangle beside the first in just the same way.

'What are you doing?' Shaun demanded. The Doctor didn't answer. *Is he mad?* thought Sylvia. *He'll get cut to pieces in the crossfire out there…*

Gingerly the Doctor pushed the first rectangle with

just the weight of his hand so that it not only slid into the hall but slightly down towards the front door.

Instantly, the bullets from the soldiers stopped flying down the hall. But death rays still came zapping against the rectangle. The Doctor pushed the second glowing rectangle out into the hall and then edged it down along the hallway towards the kitchen, where the other monsters had massed. The blue energy blasts couldn't get past it either, although she could hear both sides still firing non-stop.

Sylvia realised at last what he was doing. He'd made a safe passage towards …

Oh no. 'Absolutely not,' Sylvia informed the Doctor.

By way of reply, he grabbed her hand, and Rose's, and pushed them into the hall. Shaun took Donna's and almost dragged her out of the living room.

And they all found themselves in the battlezone that was the hallway.

Sylvia looked at both shields in astonishment and, she had to admit, slight admiration.

Neither shield was perfect – the human soldier's bullets were chipping bits away from the first, and the alien bug things' ray guns were leaving scorch marks on the second, but she and the others were safe from being hit – for now.

'Upstairs,' the Doctor barked from the living room doorway. 'Up, up, up.' Then a firm look at Sylvia. '*Now!*'

Sylvia followed Shaun up after Rose and Donna.

Then Shaun yelled above the pitched battle din back into the room: 'Come on, the Meep!'

With a high-pitched scream, the Meep scuttled out

and bounded up the stairs like an oversized rabbit. Sylvia cringed as it brushed past her, scrabbling to join Rose at the top of the stairs. But what about the Doctor? She heard a kind of electronic warble as the screen keeping back the bullets collapsed. The gunfire's volume jumped as the Doctor hurtled across the hall, just as the second shield fell apart too in a volley of sizzling blue rays.

The Doctor was already pelting up the stairs. He took Sylvia's hand, almost yanking her off her feet.

'This way,' he said, pointing upwards.

Outside in the back garden, two Wrarth Warriors, unfazed by the UNIT bullets that just bounced off their chitinous plated armour, were joined by two more emerging from the wreck of the Nobles' kitchen.

'Meep detected,' one of the newcomers reported. 'Second level.'

All four raised their blasters and fired straight up and blew a massive hole in the first-floor wall, ignoring the bricks and blocks that crashed down and bounced off them.

The one who had spoken then flexed its shoulders and four powerful wings unfurled. Soon the wings were fluttering so fast they were just a blur, and the Wrarth Warrior rose effortlessly into the sky, coming level with the hole that had just been made.

With the retreat of the Wrarth Warriors, the UNIT soldiers led by Colonel Chan swarmed into the Nobles' hallway. The warriors were no longer their target.

'Find the Meep!' yelled Chan.

Vaughan and her patrol reached the first floor and were greeted by the flying Wrarth Warrior.

Human eyes met Wrarth eyes.

The soldiers opened fire, but so too did the Wrarth Warrior. Bolts of blue energy blasted through Vaughan and her squad. As they fell to the floor, Colonel Chan hung back, the intelligence inside him plotting his next move.

The Doctor's party had reached the second floor now, and he was looking up at a hatchway in the ceiling leading up to the attic.

Donna and Shaun looked at one another. 'They just blew our house up,' Donna was wailing. The Meep added to the noise; they hadn't stopped their own unique kind of wailing for the past few minutes.

Rose yanked on a string; the hatch flipped upwards and a ladder dropped down.

The Doctor beamed his approval. 'Up you go,' he said, 'fast as you can.'

Rose smiled back and started to climb.

Sylvia noticed the look between them and, as Shaun and Donna scaled the ladder after Rose, she grabbed the Doctor's arm. 'That's my only granddaughter,' she hissed. 'Don't you dare do to her what you did to Donna. You understand me?'

'Sylvia,' he said, 'I am trying to save her. All of you. Now, get up there.'

With a final poisonous glare, Sylvia followed the others.

Rose reappeared at the hatch, holding out her arms.

With some effort, the Doctor picked up the Meep – who felt surprisingly muscular under the coat of fur – and hefted them above his head into Rose's outstretched arms.

She hauled the Meep into the attic. Then the Doctor nipped up the ladder himself, pulled it up behind him and slammed down the hatch.

Across the road, Fudge was having the time of his life. While he could hear his own family downstairs yelling about what was going on outside, he was just recording it all for posterity, leaning out of his open bedroom window so he could take it all in.

'Basically,' he was shouting down the phone at Shazza, in between sending her photos, 'there are these army guys in helmets, shooting their way into Rose's place. Don't worry, I think she's got away into the attic. It's really loud and busy and – oh hang on.'

Fudge stared down into the street. One of the visored soldiers who had run back out of Rose's house was pointing further down left, past the new blockade of cars, down towards number 1, where Bachelor Road met Kavanagh Street.

'Hostiles at West 95, engage,' Fudge clearly heard the soldier yell.

At which point the soldiers that weren't already lying on the ground around Rose's front door all looked to their left and opened fire.

'Oh my god, Shazza,' he reported. 'Those bug-aliens I told you about, they're down the bottom of the road, shooting at the soldiers!'

Then another noise and off to the right, behind the original blockade down by Mrs Higgins's place, more armoured cars arrived.

These new soldiers weren't wearing helmets, but normal berets. Normal! Ha!

A guy with a black turban tied to his head was getting ready to help the visored guys and— 'Hang on, Shazza. Oh my god, the visored guys are shooting at the new guys. That's mad. They're shooting in both directions. Idiots!' Fudge allowed himself a quick facepalm at their stupidity and then started taking more photos for Shazza to see.

Fudge heard the guy with the turban shouting into his radio thing: 'Confirm, rogue UNIT troops under hostile control. This is a Code Red! Open fire!'

And now his guys were shooting at the guys with visors, who were shooting back not only at them but also at the bug-aliens at the other end of the road.

Fudge noticed the beret bunch didn't seem to be shooting at the visored troops so much as trying to box them in. Like they didn't want to hurt them, just contain them.

Suddenly a car exploded, shooting up into the air like something out of *GTA*. It turned into a massive fireball before crashing down into the middle of the street again, knocking a couple of the visored guys to the ground.

Utter madness.

And brilliant.

'Don't tell Rose, Shazza, but her gran's Kia just got turned into scrap metal! I dunno who hit it, the visor soldiers, the beret bunch or the bug-aliens. I bet it was the visor soldiers. They haven't got a clue what they are doing.'

One of the parked army Land Rovers burst into flames too.

Fudge felt the heat and yanked his head back in. 'That was too close,' he said.

He peeked out again, to see all the soldiers with visors on were now out of the battle, lying on the ground, taken out by the bug-aliens.

And the other soldiers had fallen back behind their smouldering vehicles.

He took another photo. The *Herald* would pay a fortune for these.

In spite of everything, Fudge allowed himself a smile. That DS-E controller for his PlayStation was as good as his now!

The Doctor was standing in the Nobles' attic with the others. He walked towards the breeze-block wall that separated this attic from the one inside number 21.

He looked at the assembled family and the Meep, holding up his sonic screwdriver for them all to see.

'Now this is a sonic screwdriver. And if it's good at one thing, it's resonating concrete.' He pressed the sonic against the wall and switched it on. Instantly the wall shook and all the dust between the blocks started pouring out onto his shoes. After a few seconds, he gave the wall a shove and, sure enough, it crumbled away.

'That's not actually concrete,' Shaun said. 'It's mortar and—'

'Yes, thank you, Bob the Builder,' said Donna, before

tapping the Doctor's shoulder. 'Skinny man, you're not bad.'

Caught up in the moment, the Doctor beamed with pride. 'Awww, d'you think?'

Before Donna could say anything else, Sylvia Noble charged between them, almost dragging Donna with her. 'No, she does not,' she snapped. Then, echoing the Doctor earlier, she added, 'Come on,' and led the group into next door's attic.

This space had actually been converted into a bedroom, with a separate toilet and a Velux window.

Shaun looked around. 'We should do this to ours.'

'Before or after they knock down the rest of our house?' asked Donna as the Doctor all but disintegrated the wall into number 19.

They tiptoed through that attic (still an attic) and, once again, down came a wall and they were in number 17. Another wall went and they were in number 15.

'Billy's?' asked the Doctor.

'Billy's,' confirmed Shaun.

They dropped down from the attic and started down the stairs, typical of terraced houses, identical in layout to Shaun and Donna's place, except it hadn't been shot to pieces by aliens and possessed UNIT soldiers.

They passed a living room – and the Doctor looked in.

Sat in a huge armchair with, going by the vinyl sleeve next to him, some band called Red Dawn's *Flying High* leaking from his headphones, was a man. He was fast asleep in front of a television, mutely running an old black-and-white *Lassie* film. 'Billy,' mused the Doctor, then looked at Shaun. 'Billy MacPherson?'

Shaun nodded. 'How'd you know?'

'I met a mate of his earlier.' The Doctor felt a shiver; there was no shortage of coincidence, this day – and he doubted that was coincidence either. 'Come on, then!' He opened the front door and peered out.

Blue bolts of energy were still flying from right to left and the UNIT soldiers returning fire were some way away, behind vehicles. The Doctor noted that all the visored ones lay crumpled in the streets.

He spotted a young lad watching from opposite and made a gesture that suggested he get out of sight. But the boy ignored him.

Parked on the opposite side of the road to Billy MacPherson's, just as Shaun had said, was the black taxicab.

'Can I have the keys?' the Doctor asked Shaun.

'I drive that, mate.'

The Doctor made a point of looking all around. 'Through battlefields?'

'That cab's our livelihood!'

'Let him do it,' said Donna behind, her voice softer.

Shaun didn't look convinced. 'He's insane.'

'Maybe.' Donna pointed at the carnage everywhere. 'And maybe that's just what we need.'

With a sigh, Shaun passed the keys to the Doctor.

The Doctor darted across the road, opened the cab doors and waved them across one by one.

Rose dragged the Meep in first. They both clambered into the back of the cab but stayed down on the floor, leaving room on the back seats for Shaun and Sylvia. Donna pulled down the little extra seat and perched on it, her back to the glass partition.

Before the Doctor got in, he stopped in the street, ducking as blue energy from a Wrarth gun zoomed over his head. He had found Colonel Chan lying there, having been hit in the chest presumably, although there was no obvious mark.

He felt for a pulse.

He moved to another body and did the same.

'What?' he muttered.

He thought he was being quiet, but clearly not as, half a street away, a Wrarth Warrior swung round and fired at him.

For a moment the Wrarth Warrior's unblinking red eyes and the Doctor's startled blue ones locked.

'Meep located,' shouted the Wrarth Warrior. 'Meep within the vehicle. Stop the Meep!'

The Doctor scrambled into the driver's seat and started the cab's engine.

'Get us out of here,' Donna yelled as the Wrarth Warriors turned as one to face the vehicle, guns raised

And the Doctor sped towards them, ignoring Sylvia and the Meep's yelling as he did so.

Forced into evasive action, the Wrarth Warriors didn't have long to fire. Their wings carried them up a few metres into the air as the taxi roared past beneath them. As it zoomed away, a couple of blue beams bounced off the rear window and hit the tarmac. The Wrarth Warriors gave chase, but the Doctor managed to lose them by taking a number of back streets and alleyways. Soon they were far away from the battle of Bachelor Road.

'Oh. My. God,' Donna finally breathed out. 'That was mad.'

'You did it,' Shaun said, voice full of admiration. 'You really do have the Knowledge!'

'We're alive,' Rose said, hugging the Meep.

'Meep, meep,' the Meep agreed.

The Doctor looked in the rear-view mirror and saw Sylvia staring at him.

He readied himself for another telling off.

She silently mouthed, 'Thank you,' and smiled.

But the Doctor wasn't smiling. He was thinking of Colonel Chan lying in the street. He was thinking of how easy it was getting past those Wrarth Warriors. He was thinking about the pitched gun battle in the Nobles' hallway that went on and on with no one really winning or losing.

'Either we escaped,' he muttered, 'or we've got things very, very wrong.'

He glanced again in the rear-view mirror, and could see Rose's back as she hugged the Meep.

And his eyes met the Meep's eyes. Big, round, oh-so-grateful, butter-wouldn't-melt eyes.

Yes, he thought. *Something is very wrong indeed*.

As he drove, the Doctor carefully took his sonic screwdriver from out of his pocket and laid it down on the dashboard.

Very faintly, not enough that anyone in the back could see, it was pulsating slightly, its blue glow getting stronger or dimmer depending which roads he turned down, like a strange sort of sat-nav, guiding him somewhere.

In the back of the cab, he could hear Shaun, Sylvia and Rose discussing the damage to the house, shocked, forlorn, trying to make light of things. Not Donna, though. Donna was just staring straight ahead, as if she was studying the route the Doctor took the cab.

Or studying him.

After about ten minutes' driving, the cab was somewhere around the back of Highgate Cemetery, just on the edge of Kentish Town. The Doctor could see an underground car park ahead under an office block. The grille was down, forbidding entry, but the sonic made short work of that. The grille slowly rose, and he drove the cab down into the darkness. He reckoned they were probably about a ten-minute walk from the Millson Wagner Steelworks.

The Doctor tapped the sonic again and the overhead lights in the car park all came on, immediately silencing everyone in the back of the cab. Then he neatly parked the taxi and got out, his hand gesture suggesting that everyone else should stay put.

He opened the back door, passed Shaun his keys back, and then held a hand out to the Meep who took it and allowed itself to be led out.

Rose went to follow, but Sylvia gently held her back.

As the Doctor crossed to the bays opposite, the Meep hopped after him. He turned to face the little alien.

Then he placed his hand into his pocket and produced a tie-wig, as worn by British barristers in the law courts, and placed it on his head.

'This court is now in session,' he said gravely. He then lifted his sonic up and activated it. A single beep. 'Intercept teleport,' he added.

With a flare and a shimmer of teleportation light, two Wrarth Warriors popped into existence. They regarded the Doctor, then turned their red eyes towards the Meep and raised their guns.

The Meep gave a high-pitched, terrified scream – and Donna jumped out of the back of the cab, ignoring the Wrarth Warriors as if bug-eyed aliens were something she saw every day of her life.

'What the hell are you doing?' she demanded of the Doctor, but he just gave her a sharp look and said, 'Silence in court,' with such authority that Donna fell quiet, hanging back by the door of the cab.

Addressing the Wrarth Warriors, the Doctor pointed to their guns. 'I am invoking Shadow Proclamation Protocols 15 P and 6. Under my jurisdiction there will be no violence until such time as I deem it fit and proper, is that understood?'

There was a long pause. Then both Wrarth Warriors lowered their guns accordingly.

'Now,' the Doctor carried on, with just a small sigh of relief. 'Exhibit A. Shaun Noble's taxi. No scorch marks. Donna, can you confirm?'

Donna did as requested, looking all around the cab, touching the windows, looking at the headlights, running a hand across the tyres. Eventually she looked back at the strange court in front of her. 'No, nothing.'

'We were hit by Wrarth plasma bolts, and yet there

isn't a mark. And Colonel Chan, lying in the street, was unconscious. Not dead.' He then pointed at the Wrarth Warriors. 'Exhibit B. The Wrarth guns are stun guns. Is that correct?'

One of the Wrarth Warriors nodded, dipping slightly as his legs bent at the same time. A sign of deference perhaps. 'The guns apply a mild and harmless neural anaesthetic.' He then held his clawed arm out. 'For the record, I am Sergeant Zogroth.'

'And I am Constable Zreeg,' the second warrior added, giving a similar dip.

The Meep was giving the Doctor the biggest, most *pweeze-believe-me* eyes. 'Help! The evil Wrarth Warriors want to kill the Meep!'

'The only ones out to kill,' the Doctor continued, unfazed by the Meep's big eyes, 'were those UNIT soldiers with the swirling eyes. So, were they coming to *hurt* you, the Meep? Or were they coming to *save* you?'

Sergeant Zogroth dipped again. 'May I speak?'

The Doctor gave a slight bow. 'Address the Court.'

'The story of the Meep is a tragic tale. Their planet basked in the light of the Living Sun. Until one day, the sun went mad.'

'A Psychedelic Sun,' Constable Zreeg explained. 'Its radiation mutated all of Meepkind into cruel beasts who only lived for conquest.'

The Doctor thought back to what he'd seen under the UNIT soldier's visor. 'Their eyes. It was Solar Psychedelia!'

Sergeant Zogroth agreed. 'It renders them as maniacs.'

Constable Zreeg jabbed a claw at the Meep. 'The

Meep Army,' he said, 'captured the Galactic Council and beheaded them. Then ate them. The Shadow Proclamation summoned the Wrarth Warriors and we fought across the stars. A long and awful battle.'

Sergeant Zogroth took up the story. 'Meepkind died rather than surrender, and now only this one survives. Their leader.'

'The most cruel and despicable of all,' Zreeg added.

The Meep looked at the Doctor with their best *but-we-are-cute-and-fluffy-and-everyone-adores-us* eyes, perhaps hoping for support against this apparent slander.

Donna had now been joined by Shaun, Sylvia and Rose.

'Meep, meep,' the Meep pleaded in Rose's direction. But Rose kept her gaze fully on her parents.

'This is an unbiased court,' the Doctor declared. 'It's your turn, the Meep. Witness for the Defence. What do *you* have to say?'

The Meep fixed a stare on the Doctor, their eyes getting wider and wider. And then they smiled, showing nasty razor-sharp teeth and a slightly forked tongue. 'Oh, to hell with this,' they snapped. 'Exhibit C!'

And from some marsupial pouch within their fur, the Meep whipped out a tiny weapon, shaped like a knuckle duster, fitting precisely round their paws so only the Meep could operate it. When the Meep spoke, there was none of the childlike innocence, nothing sweet or adorable. The Meep's real voice was spiteful, angry and sarcastic, oozing the joy of a proud mass murderer. 'No stun guns for me!' they rasped. 'Just die!'

The little gun fired. Shot one sent Constable Zreeg sprawling to the ground, and the second knocked Sergeant Zogroth clean across the car park.

'Oh my god…' Donna ran forward.

'Donna, don't,' Shaun began, grabbing for her arm. But he was too slow. Seconds later, Donna was beside the Doctor and together they bent over the two prone Wrarth Warriors.

'What can we do?' asked Donna.

'I'm not sure – I don't really know the species. I can't…' He gently shook Sergeant Zogroth. 'Can you hear me?'

'Too late,' shrieked the Meep. 'My Soldiers of the Psychedelic Sun are here!'

Sure enough, UNIT jeeps swarmed into the car park, visored troops jumping out, armed to the teeth, before the vehicles had even pulled up.

'Shaun, get Rose out of here,' Donna yelled, but it was already too late. Guns clicked as their safety catches disengaged and were brought up to cover Shaun, Rose and Sylvia. The Nobles raised their hands in surrender.

The Meep snarled, the car park lights glinting off their razor teeth. 'Now I don't need to pretend any more, because I am the Beep of all Meepkind!'

Sergeant Zogroth feebly raised his clawed hand to the Doctor and Donna. 'Sergeant Zogroth regrets… retirement from active duty.' The claw dropped and his red eyes dimmed until they were black.

Donna swung round on the Meep. 'I was right all along. You *are* a monster!'

The Meep giggled and chortled. 'Yet you believed every

102

word I said. You stupid woman.' The Meep turned and looked at Rose, who stared back defiantly. 'A stupid woman with a weird child.'

Furious, Donna stood up. 'Don't you dare—'

In a flash, the Meep's knuckle-duster gun was aimed at her face.

The Doctor, still on his knees next to the dead Wrarth Warriors, quickly shot his hands up in surrender too. And then he stared straight into the Meep's eyes. 'No, no, no, no more shooting. Please.'

'Why not?'

'Because,' the Doctor said, carefully straightening his barrister's wig, 'I have last-minute evidence.' And he stood, pointing at his own chest. '*Me*. Ask yourself this, the Meep: why is there another two-hearted species on this planet? Unless I'm part of a strategy by the Wrarth Warriors to outfox you. If you kill me, and if you fail to take this family hostage as well, you'll never find out. Will you?'

The Meep's eyes widened and shrank as they considered the Doctor's words. 'Bring them,' they squeaked at last. 'Bring them all.'

The Doctor relaxed, puffing air from his cheeks in relief. 'Good. Now look: I can suggest a much better way off this planet than a Double Bladed Dagger Drive. Because believe me, that thing's going to—'

That was when a clearly recovered Colonel Chan walked up behind the Doctor and clubbed him on the back of the head with something that felt suspiciously like an automatic rifle.

And the Doctor was out like a light.

Galactic Council Massacre

Article • Talk   Read • Edit • View history • Tools^v

From *Galaxipedia*, the free omniversal encyclopedia

For the Yuletide song by the Perigosto Stix[1] inspired by this event, see Hippity Hop, Boppity Bop, Who's Next for the Chop?

The **Galactic Council Massacre,** also known as the start of the **Yarras Conflict**, was an event that signalled the end of the species, culture and history of Meepkind.

After the sun in the small Yarras solar system where MeepWorld was situated simultaneously changed its magnetic poles and endured a thermal pulse, the Living Sun was irrevocably transformed into a Psychedelic Sun. The effect on the MeepWorld's population was traumatic, driving all inhabitants insane, screaming and wailing day and night. [citation needed] Before this event, Meepkind was listed in as innocuous, socially-advanced artists and artisans, living in harmony with their planet and galaxy. After the cosmic event, the radiation meant the Meep became warlike, predatory and paranoid.[2]

After a number of skirmishes with other galactic powers, the Galactic Federation sent five leaders from the G-Council,[3] representing different planets within the local galaxy. Meepkind immediately executed the representatives upon their arrival and, according to some reports [citation needed] skinned, cooked and ate their corpses.

This attack on the sovereignty of the Galactic Council resulted in an emergency request to the Shadow Proclamation to involve their judiciary armies, led by the Wrarth Warriors, to intervene and cauterize the advancement of Meepkind.

Overseen by <u>Judge Scraggs GC</u>, the Wrarth Warriors quickly supressed the entire planet and placed it under martial law. Tragically, and unforeseen by all the experts, behaviourists and <u>Médecins Sans Frontières Galactiques</u>, on the night now referred to as <u>Psychedelia Mors Voluntaria</u>, the entire population of Meepkind simultaneously induced a <u>myocardial infarction</u> and in less than five standard space-minutes, committed self-inflicted genocide.

Rumours persist that a number of Meepkind may have become mercenaries and soldiers of fortune, after escaping the planet moments before the myocardial incident occurred, including the <u>Most High Beep of all the Meeps</u>,[4] but these reports have never been substantiated.

[1] Wrokzbirgg, G: *Cosmic Yuletide Rock n Roll Hits, 4th Ed.*, p 563

[2] Thripstead, Gustous R: *Flora and Fauna of the Universe*, p 3682

[3] '<u>Who Were the Infamous Five?</u>' – retrieved from *Daily Nebulous*

[4] Thripstead, Gustous R: *Flora and Fauna of the Universe*, p 3697: 'Beep was a title, a rank, not an individual's name. During the Yarras Conflict it came to mean "Vicious Warlord" and was bestowed upon the Most High Beep of all the Meeps. Its origins however can be found in the Old Language of Meep Antiquities: it translates as *"Glorious leader whose job is to be most perfectly round, like planets, moon, suns, pseudanthium and cake."*'

6

Countdown to Apocalypse

'Who are you?'

The question wasn't so much asked as barked. But as the Doctor snapped into consciousness – and owww, with a very sore back-of-head, thank you very much – he had to admit, it surprised him how long it had taken Donna to ask that particular question.

Quite how he should answer it, he wasn't sure.

'What's your name?' Donna continued.

The Doctor was tempted to buy time by doing a Donna: answer one question with another three. Like, where were they? Were they prisoners? And who had hit him?

He didn't ask any of them out loud, however, because the dead faces of the two Wrarth Warriors swam back into his mind's eye. He decided to focus his energy on getting the Meep sorted out before any more avoidable deaths were on his conscience.

'I'm just passing by,' the Doctor muttered.

Donna changed tack and turned to her mum. 'Do you know him?'

'No,' lied Sylvia, a simple answer but delivered with

enough conviction that even the Doctor thought she might have been telling the truth.

Donna, however, clearly knew her mother better. 'You act like you know him,' she argued. 'Ever since he arrived, it's like …'

She stopped talking. As if she had the words but they wouldn't come out. Or couldn't.

'It's my fault,' Donna finally muttered. 'I'm so stupid.'

Without any hesitation, and full of genuine love, Shaun told his wife, 'No, you're not.'

'I am, though.' Donna settled back against the canvas of the truck's hood, as the Doctor got up and sat next to Rose. 'We could be living far away from here. Monte Carlo. Or Switzerland.' Then the frown, the confusion was back, etched into her face, almost as if it hurt her physically. She hugged her daughter. 'You'd be safe, Rose.'

'I'm okay,' Rose assured her.

'But it's all my fault. I gave all that lottery money away.'

'Why?' the Doctor asked.

Donna gazed forward, into space, as if remembering, but not quite understanding. 'Because I thought there are places … out there. Where people are in danger, and in pain, and fear.' She shook her head in disappointment. 'I can help, I thought. It just felt like the sort of thing he would do.'

For a second no one said anything. The Doctor and Sylvia exchanged a scared look.

'Who?' the Doctor prodded, trying to sound as casual as possible, despite Sylvia's face full of fear.

108

He pictured Donna again in the TARDIS, breaking down. *Binary, binary, binary.*

Donna's mouth was working, trying to form a word, or a sound, or something.

But nothing came out.

Sylvia watched in terror.

Rose and Shaun watched in confusion.

The Doctor just watched, looking for any sign, the exact moment he needed to step in and distract her.

The distraction came not from Donna but from the truck braking extraordinarily sharply, jolting the prisoners in the back slightly.

A second later and the canvas was tugged back, exposing them all to the cold air. They were parked exactly where the Doctor had first clambered into the other truck, outside the steelworks.

Guns were aimed at them by ranks of visored soldiers, and the Doctor raised his hands.

As if it was something she did every day, Donna did the same, and Sylvia, Rose and Shaun slowly followed her lead.

Colonel Chan was there, Sergeant Vaughan next to him. Neither of them had their faces hidden now.

It was the first time Donna, Rose and Shaun had seen the psychedelic eyes that possessed the soldiers.

Sylvia threw the Doctor a look and he smiled weakly. He could tell she was scared, not just by the soldiers and their strange eyes, but by the way Donna was starting to react to things instinctively. She might not know why she was doing it, but she was falling back into the ease of dealing with weird alien things, behaving as she had pre-metacrisis.

Once the Meep is sorted, I'll go, he swore to himself. *Never, ever come back to London in the twenty-first century if need be.*

Anything to save Donna. To save his friend.

But the Meep had to be dealt with first.

Chan led the group back through the steelworks and towards the blast furnace chamber.

As they all stepped into it, the Doctor found he was admiring the changes.

The Meep's cobalt spaceship had been expertly repaired. The gash in the side had been patched up. The propulsion units, the engines, were being rebuilt and customised. A number of people in safety clothing and welding masks were busy making sure the ship was back in pristine condition.

The Doctor knew that under all the visors and masks, their eyes would swirl with solar-psychedelic energies.

The Meep had an army now.

One man was adjusting a series of heavy-duty coaxial cables. These ran from the base of the ship to a three-panelled control desk, quite some way away, near the stairs that led up to the offices.

Even though the controls would no doubt have been alien in design, someone was standing there, operating the controls in preparation for what was coming. The Meep's new Chief Technician.

There was no visor or mask to hide his face, and his eyes were very visibly swirling with light. The Doctor felt deflated as he recognised the Meep's latest slave recruit.

Poor Stew Ferguson had never made it back to his mate Billy, to wake him up and tell him everything he'd missed.

So, the Doctor mused, the Meep didn't land in the Millson Wagner Steelworks at random. It had been a deliberate choice, somewhere with the resources to mend the creature's spaceship.

He was knocked out of his reverie by Sylvia nudging his elbow and directing him to look to the right.

Four UNIT soldiers were entering the main area. They carried twisted girders on their shoulders, on top of which was a throne, built from other bits of broken and melted metal found around the steelworks.

In front of the throne stood the Meep, clearly enjoying being carried by their human slaves. The Meep gave an evil giggle and then yelled out to the assembled throng: 'Hail to the Meep!'

Apart from the welders and the four carrying the litter, everyone else in thrall to the Psychedelic Sun stopped what they were doing and, as one, clamped their fists to their chests and responded simultaneously, 'Hail to the Most High!'

'Human scum!' the Meep continued. 'Behold my vessel to the stars! Technology far beyond your tiny, grasping minds!'

The Doctor stepped forward and addressed the Meep. 'I name this ship the Delusions of Grandeur!'

The Meep just smiled, bearing their razor-sharp teeth.

The Doctor ignored this and carried on. 'You can't fire those engines, not from here!'

The Meep giggled. 'Oh, why not?'

'Because,' the Doctor explained, as quickly yet patiently as he could, 'a Dagger Drive gets its energy by stabbing down.' He pointed to the ground beneath the spaceship's engines. 'To gain sufficient thrust to break orbit, it would need to extract about five miles square. That's a whole lot of London Town, stabbed and burned.' He regarded the Meep from under angry, hooded eyes. 'Used up as fuel.'

Rose breathed out. 'Nine million people …'

'A great day for Meepkind,' the Meep chortled. 'The start of a new reign of terror as the Meep returns to the stars for revenge.' It paused for effect, before adding, 'Oh, and feasting!' Then the Meep pointed at the Chief Technician aka Stew Ferguson. 'Activate the initialisers!'

Stew pressed a button and twisted a dial. 'Initialisers activated,' he droned.

The spaceship lit up, glittering with external sensor lights.

'Brandish the gravity stanchions,' squealed the Meep.

'Gravity stanchions brandished,' Stew confirmed, and the stanchions at the base of the spaceship shook and then retracted.

'Calibrate the flight deck!' the Meep trilled.

'Flight deck calibrated,' was the immediate obedient reply.

At the very top of the pointed cone of the cockpit, pointing up into the sky, a series of internal lights burst into life.

The Meep waved over Colonel Chan and Sergeant Vaughan.

'Now, take the prisoners on board, then I'll decide which one I'll eat first.' Chan and Vaughan bowed and walked towards the Doctor's group as the Meep warbled one last command to the enslaved workers. 'Hail to the Meep!' Of course, everyone dutifully slammed their fists to their chests again and responded with a rousing chorus: 'Hail to the Most High!'

Chan and Vaughan escorted the Doctor and the Noble family over to a rickety metal cage attached to a lift that went up to each of the different levels of the steelworks. The door to the spaceship was on the third floor, and the Doctor calculated the odds of overcoming the soldiers and escaping in the time it would take to walk out of the lift, along the walkway and then over to the ramp into the ship.

On his own, it might just prove possible. But with the Nobles to keep safe too, he knew he stood no chance.

'In,' Chan snapped, and they dutifully shuffled into the lift cage.

Chan marched away as Vaughan and another soldier joined them inside and activated the lift. It rose up.

The Doctor checked on Donna. She was quiet and watchful; starting to behave like the Donna of old. Exactly as she shouldn't be.

After a couple of minutes that seemed to last hours, the lift stopped on the third floor.

Sergeant Vaughan pulled open the doors to the lift...

And sat there, in her chair, was Shirley Anne Bingham.

'Evening folks,' she said – and from the arms of her wheelchair, darts shot out, hitting each soldier in the neck. Vaughan and her compatriot were unconscious before they hit the walkway.

'Shirley Anne Bingham! Oh, you utter star,' the Doctor beamed. 'You've got weapons in your wheelchair!'

'We all have.' Shirley winked. 'Well,' she added urgently, 'come on!'

The Doctor led the charge, closely followed by the Nobles. Shirley brought up the rear with a nifty turn of speed in her chair across the uneven metal walkway. But they all came quickly to a stop with the spaceship to the left of them: ahead was a dead end. To their right stood a heavy-duty steel door, like something from a submarine.

'Right, you lot,' Shirley addressed the Nobles and pointed to the steel door. 'You can get out through that, down the corridor and towards the fire escape.' She then looked at the Doctor. 'And you need to get to Engine Control. But the portside is guarded and there's no obvious way around to it.'

'So, what do we do?' the Doctor asked.

Shirley patted her wheelchair. 'I don't just fire darts, mate.'

At which point she yanked up the arms of the chair, revealing miniature missiles. She fired them, and the dead end ceased being a dead end and became a very large access point to more walkways beyond.

She threw a look at the Nobles, who were astonished at what she had just done. 'Don't stand there, run. I'll fight them off at the lift.' She jerked her head at Shaun, who immediately started wrestling the big door open. As he did so, Shirley added a 'Good luck!'

Donna was staring at the hole in the wall, and then back at the Doctor, a curious look on her face. However, before she could say anything, Shaun grabbed her hand and dragged her away, yelling, 'Donna, come on!'

And they were gone.

Below, Chan and his soldiers started to react to the explosion with yells and orders but. for the Doctor and Shirley, it was a quiet moment of bonding. And understanding.

'Was that Donna Noble?' she asked reverently.

He just nodded.

The lift they had come up in started to descend some way behind them. 'Go,' Shirley snapped, and the Doctor shot off through the newly-formed hole in the wall.

Sylvia was in second place in the family group, following Shaun down the corridor as he'd been instructed. He then heaved open the metal-meshed door which led to the fire escape and out into the open, and potential safety, behind the steelworks.

Sylvia was just passing Shaun, who was holding the door open for everyone, when there was a commotion behind her. Donna suddenly grabbed Shaun and kissed him.

'I'm sorry, darling,' Donna said. 'I love you.' She then kissed Rose's forehead and pushed her and Shaun towards Sylvia.

'Mum! What are you doing?' asked Rose.

Sylvia had guessed. And so, judging by his reaction, had Shaun.

'Donna, you can't—' he started to say, but Donna had already slammed the door shut on them, pulling the bar across the metal-mesh door. trapping herself inside.

She stared at them through the mesh, putting her fingers through, so Shaun could touch them.

Sylvia felt sick. After all this time, Donna was back being Donna. Sylvia felt more scared by that realisation than anything else over the last half an hour.

'Take Rose,' Donna told Shaun. 'Take her ten miles away, somewhere safe. I love you, Shaun, but if the Doctor can't save the city, we're all going to die.'

Shaun opened his mouth and closed it again, no words coming.

Donna just smiled. A huge smile, sad but determined, that Sylvia hadn't seen in ages. In about fifteen years.

And then she was gone, running back the way they had come.

'Donna!' Shaun yelled. He shook the mesh door, but it was no use.

Sylvia came over and stopped him, sighing sadly. 'She called him "Doctor".' Sylvia knew now that there was nothing she or Shaun could do, except follow Donna's orders and get Rose to safety.

Taking Rose's hand, Sylvia led her down the stairs, an angry Shaun following on.

Back inside the blast furnace chamber, the Doctor was dashing along gantries and walkways, moving around obstacles almost like a gymnast.

Ahead of him, as Shirley had promised, was a huge

door in the side of the spaceship, leading to the Engine Control Room.

He sonicked it as he ran, and it slid upwards to allow him through.

He skidded to a halt inside and took a deep breath. 'Engine Control Room, check,' he muttered. It was very wide and very high. Every millimetre of wall was covered in buttons, switches, dials, screens, writing so alien even he couldn't read it. A million controls, the busiest he'd ever seen, loads of lights flicking on and off.

Where to begin? Sabotage was all very well, but it usually helped if you had an idea what was sabotageable, and what was actually the self-destruct button. Despite what other people often believed, very rarely did things come with a helpful, palm-sized button marked SELF-DESTRUCT, so who knew what might happen if he began randomly wrecking things.

As he spun round on his heel, trying to work things out, his thinking was interrupted by puffing and panting that certainly wasn't his own.

'That's enough running,' said Donna Noble in the entranceway. 'Blimey.' Then she looked around the vast room and all its flickering technology. 'Blimey,' she said again.

The Doctor's hearts sank. 'No, no, no, I told you to go.'

Conflicted, the Doctor was torn between wanting to hug her and wanting to scream at her. He knew that if she remembered him, their time together: BANG! Brain gone. Like a human bomb...

Binary, binary, binary...

Standing inside this spaceship was more likely to trigger that than anything else.

He shook his head, angrily. 'Just don't… Gaaaah! I've no time for this.' He swivelled round, trying to convince himself he could do what needed to get done. 'I've got it,' he repeated. 'I've got it, I've got it… You just stay there, I'm fine.'

High above the Doctor and Donna, situated in the pointed noise cone of the ship was the flight deck. Sat in the pilot's seat, strapped in, ready to take off, was the Meep.

They were tapping at tiny controls designed for their unique puckered fingertips. 'Maximise petrolinks and combustible hyperlines,' squeaked the Meep, sitting back in satisfaction. All was going well.

Of course, it could be better – yes, there ought to be some pomp, some ceremony. Give these pitiful Earth creatures a reason to live for about, oh, another three minutes before the Meep's spaceship blasted off and reduced London to red hot slag.

The Meep tapped an intercom button.

'Hail to the Meep!' they shouted.

Sylvia Noble had lost an argument. Truth be told, Shaun had lost it too, although his heart hadn't been in the argument in the first place; but as a dutiful dad, he had at least gone through the motions of agreeing with Sylvia.

Rose, however, had won.

As a result, the entire Noble family were now back in

the blast furnace chamber, on the ground floor, just below the office area, to the right of where the hypnotised man in the janitor's uniform was directing events from the Meep's big control console.

They had been joined by the lady in the wheelchair who had saved them upstairs earlier – Shirley, the Doctor had called her.

'We were going to go,' Sylvia hissed, 'but …'

Shirley waved her aside. 'Donna went after the Doctor, yes? I can see she's not with you.'

Sylvia nodded. 'She must be in that spaceship thing now. With him!'

Further sotto conversation was halted, when over the speaker system, they all heard the Meep's shout. Everyone in the area bar Shirley and the Noble family immediately responded with a triumphant 'Hail to the Most High.'

Shaun looked at his remaining family. 'We can't get out. We're trapped.'

'What can we do?' Rose asked Sylvia and Shaun.

Sylvia and Shaun had no answer.

The Meep was busy tapping at more controls, watching the readings flooding in from the control console down near the base of the rocket.

That control unit had cost quite a few Galactic Credits – especially to build in the safeguards that ensured it would be the very last thing to be destroyed (no point in using it to power the ship's take-off if it got vaporised thirty seconds before it was needed). But the Meep was ultimately willing to make the sacrifice, letting it be atomised along with its user after all the other controlled humans had burned to dust and the Meep was safely en-route for the stars.

It was a shame, thought the Meep, that from up here, as the ship took off and G-force kicked in, they would be unable to actually see the humans die in shrieking agony. But, sometimes even the Most High had to sacrifice fun for expediency.

'Primary Ignition Signature installed and …' The Meep stabbed another button. '… deadlock sealed.'

Some way below the Meep, in the Engine Control Room, the Doctor was literally climbing the walls, sonicking controls, hoping some minor sabotage would be enough to slow the Meep down and give him a chance to save all the innocent people outside.

Suddenly the Doctor felt the sonic vibrate and then give out a puff of smoke, as if it had been hit. Which it had – a reversal of energy from one of the controls he'd been sonicking.

'The controls have been deadlocked,' he smarted, shoving the useless sonic back inside his jacket and dropping back to the floor.

Over by the door, Donna frowned. 'What does that mean?'

'It means,' the Doctor replied, hitting every button he could reach, 'I'm going to have to do everything by hand.'

The Meep was counting. They counted the digits on their left paw with the right. Then they counted the digits on their right paw with the left. Upon reaching the final digit, the Meep grinned, bearing those razor-sharp teeth once again in a grimace of joy.

'Time to bisect the maxifold!'

The Meep flicked one more switch.

Down in the Engine Control Room, the Doctor was tracing a link between three buttons with his finger when he heard a sound.

A whirring. A heavy, unpleasant, whirring.

He spun round. Donna was still by the door. He was by the furthest controls from her.

Sliding down the centre of the Engine Control Room was a triangular glass partition – wide at the base, thinner at the top where it met the ceiling – which would separate them from one another.

'No, no, no…' The Doctor threw himself under the slowly descending screen so he was next to Donna. He started hitting controls by her knees.

The partition continued downwards.

He realised that if it wasn't those controls, and it wasn't these controls, then it had to be some *other* controls over there. He rolled back under the partition and tried hitting a set of buttons he hadn't tried before.

Nothing.

The glass partition hit the floor with a heavy thump. 'It's okay,' he called to Donna, now cut off from him. 'I can still do it, even with only half the room. It's fine!'

'Let me help,' Donna suggested from her side of the bisected room.

Binary, binary, binary…

'No,' the Doctor said, slightly more sharply than he intended. 'You can't get involved. You mustn't and… Aargghhh.' He was furious. He looked at Donna.

He had to risk it.

But should he?

Binary, binary, binary…

'Those blue switches,' he snapped, pointing near her left shoulder. 'Flick them down.'

Donna Noble started flicking switches.

Donna Noble had always been good at flicking switches.

Switches to operate the Magnetron. Switches to operate the Lux Library. Switches to operate the TARDIS …

Binary, binary, binary…

On the spaceship's flight deck, the Meep gave one last evil chuckle.

'Activate the Dagger Drive!'

The Meep slammed both paws down hard on the controls. 'And burn, you city of the damned!'

The destruction of London began instantly…

Not for the first time that night, Sylvia Noble wished she and her family were anywhere else but the Millson Wagner steelworks. Rose had insisted they come back to save Donna but, right now, Sylvia was pretty sure it was the three of them that needed rescue.

Less than ten metres away from them was the base of that space rocket and it was doing things that Sylvia

122

was pretty sure weren't going to be good for anyone. She could feel great waves of heat washing across the blast furnace area.

Then suddenly the whole ground shook and Sylvia saw Shirley's chair involuntarily roll forward. Rose grabbed her before any of the possessed soldiers and workers – now all standing to attention on the upper gantries – could spot her. The only person on the ground floor with them was the hypnotised janitor guy operating the Meep's three-panelled control unit; he reminded Sylvia of Jean Michel-Jarre at that Docklands concert Geoff had taken her to, years ago. The shaking got steadily worse, and Sylvia watched in horror as cracks appeared in the ground. Seconds later, scalding steam started to leak upwards, followed by the first glowing bubbles of what looked like lava.

The only area untouched by the cracks was the floor around the three-panelled control unit itself. Rose and Shaun started to creep over there, and Sylvia followed, urged forward by Shirley. If anyone noticed them, they didn't show it, gazing up at the nosecone of the rocket like it was their god.

Sylvia felt no safer. After all, those cracks were spreading further and further outside the blast furnace chamber, like a red-hot molten spider's web. Eventually London would disappear into the cracks ...

Taking Sylvia's whole world with it.

Sylvia was right. That red web of lava was zig-zagging not just across north London but into the city, and blazing east and west from its epicentre at the steelworks.

Even the Thames was no barrier to the power unleashed by the Dagger Drive – bridges crumbled, and the river itself started to steam and boil as lava bubbled across the riverbed and into south London.

Tower blocks began to shake; weaker ones collapsed. Buildings covered in scaffolding, waiting for builders to return to work with the morning light, were freed from their steel embrace as, across the city, thousands of heavy metal pipes and wooden walkways crashed onto the cars and roadways below.

Emergency signals sounded from millions of phones in unison, like the horn blast heralding judgement day. People woke to watch in horror as lava began to bubble into their roads and avenues and crescents.

Beyond London too, in the home counties, the vibrations were felt. Some experts believed that within a couple of hours the entire United Kingdom could be facing devastation, whilst London itself would be entirely erased: a massive crater of lava where the most crowded city in the nation had once stood proud.

Sat in the pilot's seat on the flight deck of their spaceship, imagining the destruction below and beyond, the Meep sat cackling with unrestrained glee.

Long fingers started tippity-tapping away at the flight controls, preparing to convert all that energy into propulsion for the craft.

'All hail the Most High,' they chortled away. 'All hail me!'

* * *

A couple of metres below the Meep, Donna faced the Doctor through the glass partition that separated them.

She could still not quite comprehend who the Doctor was or how she knew him. But she felt certain that it made sense that they were here together, at the end of everything.

The Doctor pressed his head against the glass. 'If there was anything else I could do ...'

'You would,' Donna finished for him.

'There's only one thing left,' he said quietly.

'Then do it,' implored Donna.

The Doctor lifted his head again, staring again into that face. That amazing, brilliant, wonderful face of Donna Noble.

Images swarmed through his memories – Donna in a wedding dress, standing in the TARDIS control room, barking at him. At Adipose Industries, pointing at her own face in joy at seeing him again, miming a catch-up in front of aliens. Her fury at being unable to save the people of Pompeii from history. Listening to Ood-song. Sontarans. Hath. Vashta Narada. Daleks. Davros. The metacrisis. Davros jolting everything into Donna's mind with his electrical blaster. Donna saving the universe and then losing her world, becoming a Donna he didn't know. Then Christmas again. Her wedding. The Lottery ticket he'd bought with her late dad's pound coin, to set her up in comfort for life; the only way the Doctor knew to apologise for everything that had happened to her simply because she'd met him.

And then all the coincidences surrounding that meeting, both back then and again last night. Strands of the cosmos, drawing together a lonely Time Lord and an amazing woman denied her place in the pantheon of universal saviours.

'Go on,' Donna was saying, shattering his reverie. 'Do it. Hurry up and do it, what are you waiting for?'

The Doctor tried to put his thoughts into words, hoping she would understand. 'I think all this coincidence was heading here. To save London from burning.' He could feel tears in his eyes. 'Cos you and I can stop this ship, together ... but it will kill you.'

There was a beat of silence as Donna digested this. Then she did that most Donna Noble of Donna Noble things. She simply shrugged.

'Okay,' she said, as if it were the most normal thing she'd heard all week.

'You. Will. Die.' The Doctor needed her to understand.

'Mate, my daughter's down there somewhere. And it's not even just Rose. It's nine million people.' She shrugged again. 'Who cares about me?'

'I do,' the Doctor said.

'But why?' Donna was genuinely confused; it showed all over her face. 'I'm no one.'

'No, you are not,' the Doctor raged, slamming his palms against the glass in frustration. 'Why does it have to be this?'

But it had to be. There was no other way.

Beneath this spaceship, London was moments away from dying.

He lowered his face for a second, took a deep breath then just stared at Donna. So that her eyes were the only thing he could see in the room, in the world. In the whole universe. Just Donna's eyes.

'Westerly,' he said quietly. 'Pelican. Dreams.'

Donna was sighing. 'Look I don't care what it is, all right, just go and do it, will you?'

'Tornado,' murmured the Doctor. 'Clifftops. Andante.'

'Get on with it,' said Donna. 'Come on.'

'Grief. Fingerprint. Susurration.'

And Donna stopped getting flustered. Instead she just murmured back a surprised 'Oh' as if she felt ... something.

The Doctor saw a flash of golden energy in her eyes, just for a second. Time Lord artron energy, being released from where it had been locked away to keep her safe.

'Sparrow,' the Doctor said, and Donna said it too. Then together they said, 'Dance. Mexico.'

The Doctor opened his mouth to say the final three words. But it was Donna who got there first.

'Binary. Binary. Binary,' she said.

Then the Doctor flinched as Donna's head jerked back and she stretched out her arms. Her face, her hands, her whole body was engulfed by golden Time Lord regeneration energy.

Then the blaze burned out, the energy absorbed by Donna and she dropped to her knees, looking down at the floor of the Engine Control Room.

Frustrated by the glass between them, the Doctor gazed down at her. 'Are you all right?' he breathed. 'Donna?'

Donna stood up and fixed him with a glare so cross, so

furious, so utterly livid that he actually took a step back before she even spoke.

'I gave away my money,' she enunciated, each syllable dripping with anger.

'What?'

'I gave away. All. My. Money.'

The Doctor had not expected this. 'Right,' he said finally. 'But—'

Donna was not letting this one go. 'I gave away all that lottery money, and d'you know why, Doctor?'

He shook his head.

'I gave it away to be like you! So I could be kind, so I could be nice, so I could be helpful.'

The Doctor grimaced.

Then more words tumbled out, words that no one but the DoctorDonna reborn could hope to use. 'I had a subconscious infracutaneous retrofold memory loop making me act as soft as you and give away one hundred and sixty-six million pounds.' She took a deep breath. 'A triple rollover.'

'Yes,' was the only response the Doctor could give. Then he thought she needed a little push in the right direction. 'Donna? Destruction of London?'

'Oh, I'll show you destruction, mate.'

Donna turned and walked to the controls on her side of the ship and began operating them like it was something she had done every day of her life. No hesitation. No pause to think. Just like she had in the Daleks' Crucible all those years ago when Davros had unwittingly activated the DoctorDonna in the first place.

128

'I will tripledrive the particle manifesto, overstep the umbilical feed, vindicate the cyberlines and roast the hyperfeeds like ... this!'

The Doctor was both overjoyed and terrified. Together they could save London, save the world again. Just like old times. But it would also be the last time. Because he knew that this action could only kill her.

He walked to his own controls. 'Maximise the stressfold links,' he shouted, trying to sound buoyant.

'Channel up the booster drive,' responded Donna, who was absolutely buoyant.

'Inculcate the plexidrones,' the Doctor yelled.

'And shatterfry the positrons ... oh, yes!' With a final flourish, Donna did exactly what she'd said she would do. She turned to the Doctor and smiled, so happy. Then she asked the Doctor the question that crushed him.

'How long have I got to live?'

No point in lying now. Donna deserved life, and happiness, and a future, but all the Doctor could realistically give her was the truth.

'Fifty-five seconds.'

'Best fifty-five seconds of my life.' She grinned. 'Cos I get to do this.'

And she almost casually reached out and pressed one teeny-tiny little red button.

Around them both, all the other controls shorted out and exploded. Through the carnage, the Doctor saw that Donna was still grinning.

'Donna Noble is descending!'

* * *

To the people of London, at all compass points, what happened next made no sense.

As they watched, and as millions around the world scrolled through news reports and videos and posts all over social media, the deep gashes in the streets and parklands and riverbeds of London started to close up. Red lava was sucked back inside the rents as they sealed themselves.

Other than evidence of the damage wrought by the vibrations, and an overall feeling of tropical temperatures at 4.10am on a Tuesday morning in November, it was as if nothing had happened at all.

In the Engine Control Room of the Meep's sleek and repaired cobalt-blue spaceship, the Doctor and Donna felt the vibrations lessen.

'It's working,' the Doctor said, overjoyed and deeply sad at the same time. He looked at the architect of their salvation.

Donna Noble. Triumphant.

And dying.

Sylvia Noble held Shaun and Rose close to her as the vibrations ceased.

Shirley pointed it out first. 'Look,' she said.

The red scars across the steelworks floor were already receding, back into the base of the spaceship, back into the rumbling Dagger Drive that sounded to be powering down.

Then, for no reason that Sylvia could understand, Rose

stood up. There seemed to be something wrong with her eyes.

Like they were glowing gold …

In the Engine Control Room, as the ship's power finally died, the glass partition slid back up into the ceiling and the Doctor leapt to catch Donna as she slumped forward onto her knees.

'No,' he muttered, cradling her in his arms. 'No, no, no, no …'

They were together again. For one final time.

Up at the very tip of the spaceship's nosecone, the Meep was screeching in rage. They slammed both paws down onto the comms unit.

'That two-hearted monster,' the Meep shouted. 'Guards! Get to the Engine Control Room. Kill him! Eradicate him!'

Along the gantries outside, the UNIT soldiers and workers heard this. Colonel Chan flipped up his visor, his psychedelic eyes burning with more passion than ever before.

'With me,' he said to Sergeant Vaughan and Private Jackson. 'Execute the two-hearted monster.'

The three soldiers stomped along the metal walkway, towards the sealed door to the Engine Control Room, guns cocked and ready to fire.

On the other side of that door, the Doctor was looking down into Donna's face.

Her eyes were closing. His hearts were breaking.

All over again.

'We did it,' he said gently. 'Rose is fine, she's safe. You saved her.' He forced a smile. 'You saved them all.'

Donna looked up, and then her smile turned to a frown and she painfully lifted a finger to point upwards, nearly poking him in the eye. 'Why did this face come back?'

'I don't know,' he said honestly.

'To say goodbye?' Donna suggested.

He nodded. 'Maybe.'

'That was good fun, though,' Donna said, and laughed.

The Doctor laughed too.

Then Donna's eyes closed and her head fell against his shoulder.

The Doctor knew Donna Noble was dead, and he couldn't hold back the tears. He didn't even want to. He just wept at the utter unfairness that had caused this to happen.

As the door slid upwards, the Doctor was aware in his peripheral vision of Chan and his two psychedelic-eyed troopers stepping through.

'We have orders to kill you,' Chan announced.

The Doctor was still looking at Donna's body in his arms. 'Do what you like.' His voice was steely. 'This ship isn't going anywhere. You were beaten – by the DoctorDonna.'

The Meep's voice echoed throughout the whole steelworks and into the Engine Control Room. 'Feel the wrath of the Meep! Destroy him!'

Chan and the UNIT troopers raised their guns – and then gasped and staggered.

The psychedelic light spiralled out from their eyes and dissipated in the air, along with a desperate wailing sound that just faded away with the light.

'What?' The Doctor hadn't expected that.

Chan and the others were exchanging confused looks. 'What?' the Colonel echoed.

'What?' said Donna Noble, lifting her head away from the Doctor's chest.

'You're not dead!' the Doctor whispered.

'Obviously,' Donna said. 'But how?'

Down below, operating the three-panelled control console with consummate ease, as if she'd being doing it all her life, was Rose Noble.

Sylvia and Shaun were standing nearby, watching in astonishment.

'Closing down all psychedelic lightwave emanators,' Rose said as her hands sped over the controls. 'Transferring excess power to the brokendrone pre-fixilators.'

Beside Rose, Stew Ferguson shook his head as the psychedelic light vanished from his eyes. All over the steelworks, UNIT soldiers and welders alike were doing the same, all waking from what seemed like some strange dream, unsure what had happened but knowing they were glad it was over. Whatever it was.

Shirley Anne Bingham nudged Sylvia, in admiration of Rose.

Rose stood there, a huge grin on her face. Shimmering around her like a halo was golden Time Lord energy, just as it had fired out from Donna earlier. 'Easy when you

133

know how.' Rose punched the comms control and spoke into the built-in microphone. 'Mum? Doctor? Can you hear me? I think it's safe for you to come down now. I've sorted everything out.'

Seconds later, Donna and the Doctor were standing on the ramp leading down to the gantry. Donna stared at her daughter, vestiges of the golden energy still hovering around the teenager.

The Doctor understood at last. 'Too much power for one person.' He nudged Donna's shoulder, nodding down at Rose. 'But you had a child and so the metacrisis passed down. A shared inheritance!'

'Binary, binary binary,' Donna agreed. 'Two of us. So, the potential's always been there, shining out of her!'

'Blazing out,' agreed the Doctor.

Then because her memories had been restored, Donna suddenly gasped. 'And the toys...' She closed her eyes, picturing the little blue shed, with its windows that of course resembled TARDIS windows – there was even that little chimney that looked like the TARDIS lamp. And inside, all those toys she'd watched Rose create over the last few months: Mister Spaghetti-Face – it was an Ood. Bumpy-Metal Man – a Dalek. Red Horn-Head – the Krop Tor Beast. King Rhino – a Judoon. Best Puplet – Karvanista. Metal-Head-Handles – a Cyberman. Blobby McBlobbyface – an Adipose. And, of course, Captain Potato – a Sontaran! How could she never have seen all that? Never realised they were sharing those memories?

But now it was all back in place, inside her head and

134

she was safe with that information thanks to Rose and the genes and fragments of the metacrisis they shared.

'We're binary ...' the Doctor started.

'She's not,' Donna said. 'Because you are ...'

'... Male.'

'And female.'

'And neither,' Rose said. 'And more.'

Seconds later, Rose was in Donna's arms, all hugs, and then Shaun joined in, a massive Noble family group hug.

The Doctor also went in for a hug, not with Donna and her husband and daughter, but with Sylvia.

Sylvia gave him a look that said firmly, 'Don't go there' so instead he just winked at her.

'Happy now?' he asked.

Sylvia didn't speak for a few seconds. But then she allowed a slight smile to form on her lips. 'You know what?' she said. 'My father would be impressed. I have no higher compliment.'

The Doctor grinned back, the widest grin he had ever given anyone.

Shirley nudged him. 'There's a word for you, Doctor. And that word is "jammy".'

'Jam. On toast,' he said back. Then he eased himself behind the three-panelled control unit, pausing only to take a grateful handshake from Stew Ferguson.

Then the Doctor tapped the same comms switch Rose had used just now and leaned in close. 'Calling the Meep. Calling the Meep ...'

The Meep's voice came straight back, pulsating with venom and fury. 'You forget, Doctor, I still have my ship!

135

And if I have to explode the engines and rupture this world and damn us all to hell, then I will!'

The Doctor gave a shrug and then slammed his fist down on another button.

And the top of the nosecone of the spaceship flopped aside and the pilot seat shot upwards, now turned into an ejector seat. Strapped into it, giving the loudest scream of fear, anger and outrage possible, was the Meep.

'There you go,' the Doctor told Colonel Chan as he marched over. 'All yours.' He pointed upwards and everyone watched as the ejector seat slowly came back towards them courtesy of a huge parachute, with the Meep screaming intergalactic curses that luckily no one could understand.

Where r u. U OK

> Sorry, was AFK. Did u see the fires

Course I did. Amazing

> Lava everywhere. Then it just disappeared

NE idea what happened

> Bet it was something 2 do with that stuff at Rose house. Or the aliens

Dont start

> Bug aliens. I saw them at Higgins garden gate. Had to be them.

M says no school 2mrow

Dad says hes taking me anyway. Doesnt believe in having school days off

Yr dads mean

Police just arrived at Roses. Tape everywhere. CSI Hampstead.

Get pix

7
Here We Go Again

As dawn broke over the remains of the Millson Wagner Steelworks, UNIT troopers were still keeping the reporters, the management and a number of anxious passers-by at arms' length outside the main gate.

Stew Ferguson had mentioned to the Doctor that he wondered if he'd still have a job by this afternoon, but the Doctor said he'd make sure that word got back to the owners that he was the company's hero; without Stew aiding the authorities so ably, the steelworks would be just a big crater in the ground.

Stew had then been led away by the UNIT troops to be debriefed and finally sent home.

'Well,' the Doctor said to the Noble family. 'What to do with the Meep, I wonder.'

At which point everyone was almost blinded by a bright blue light as a whole load of Wrarth Warriors teleported in from a Wrarth cruiser that had been waiting in orbit.

'Colonel Chan, Major Singh, meet the Wrarth Warriors, charged with arresting the Meep,' the Doctor smiled.

Both UNIT officers saluted and, standing some way

behind, Sergeant Vaughan and the other UNIT personnel snapped to formal attention.

The Wrarth Warriors acknowledged the human soldiers. 'May we present our credentials from the Shadow Proclamation?'

Chan knew the protocol, and took the proffered datachip, even though he had no way of doing anything with it.

'You are the Doctor?' the Wrarth asked, and the Doctor nodded. 'I am Captain Zagran.'

'An honour, Captain. I have to sadly report to you that Sergeant Zogroth and Constable Zreeg gave their lives in pursuit of bringing the Meep to justice. Along with many people of Earth.'

The Wrarth Warriors all crossed their arms in front of their chests and bowed their heads. Chan and Singh copied this, as did the Doctor.

'Their names will be included in the litany of crimes, as the Meep atones in prison for ten thousand years,' Zagran pronounced

The Meep just giggled. 'Oh, I will escape, and have my revenge.'

The Wrarth Warriors looked at each other, as if they'd heard this many times before, and it was never true.

'Oh, and beware, Doctor,' the Meep continued. 'Because there's one more thing.'

'Which is?'

'A creature with two hearts is such a rare thing. Just wait until I tell the Boss.'

At which point the blue light shimmered again, and Zagran, all his Wrarth Warriors and the evil Meep all vanished.

The Doctor was just staring where the Meep had been a second before. 'Cryptic. I hate that.' He turned to Donna and Rose. 'But we've still got to fix you two. Because the metacrisis might have slowed down, but that thing is still wrapped around your cortex—'

Donna sighed. 'Yeah, we know.'

'We know everything, thanks,' added Rose, grinning broadly.

Donna poked the Doctor's skinny chest. 'And *you* know nothing. It's a shame you're not a woman any more cos *she'd* have got it.'

Rose took up the explanation. 'Yeah, we've got all that power, but there's a way to get rid of it. Something a male-presenting Time Lord will never understand.'

Donna and Rose smiled at each other and Donna said, 'Just let it go ...'

'We *choose* to let it go ...' said Rose, taking her mum's hand. And together they drew in a deep breath and everyone watched astonished as the golden regeneration energy spiralled out from them both.

Shaun nudged the Doctor. 'Like I said, mate, how lucky am I?'

Rose and Donna were still smiling as most of the golden cloud rose higher and higher into the air and then dissipated.

Donna saw a tiny curl of gold floating near her nose. Gently, she blew on it – just as the Doctor had after his semi-regeneration had started this whole mad process – and it was reduced to atoms fading from existence.

Behind her, Shirley Anne Bingham watched as a bit of the gold dust floated towards her and she, likewise, just puffed it away, like blowing seeds off a dandelion.

A second later, there was nothing left of the artron energy, the metacrisis or any of its associated dangers.

'After all these years,' Rose said, hugging Donna, 'I'm finally me!'

Some time later, after Colonel Chan, Major Singh, Shirley Anne Bingham and everyone else had said their goodbyes, got what they needed for their reports and were generally happy for the Doctor to get out of their hair, the Time Lord and the Noble family found themselves back in Camden Lock, as London started to awaken and begin cleaning up after last night's carnage.

Donna was wondering what was going to happen to her house and all the damage.

'It's not like we've got the money to move anywhere. And I don't think Mum wants us to move in permanently. I mean now this is all working again,' Donna tapped her head, 'there could be Daleks, Ood or the odd Racnoss knocking on the front door.'

Sylvia nodded. She might love her family passionately, but 11 Wessex Avenue had been alien-free for fifteen years now, and she planned to keep it that way.

'Don't worry,' the Doctor said. 'UNIT has a great insurance policy. *Damage to Property in the Course of an Alien War.*'

142

Neither Sylvia nor Donna looked entirely convinced by this, but mentally crossed their fingers it'd turn out all right.

'And while that's being sorted out…' The Doctor led Donna to the corner of Blackcastle Passage and pointed out the waiting TARDIS.

'Don't you dare,' Sylvia said to Donna, but her daughter was already walking towards the blue box, the Doctor at her heels.

Sylvia, Rose and Shaun followed, exchanging anxious looks.

'D'you know,' Donna was saying, 'I'd love it.' She stared at the familiar old police box. Then gave the Doctor a sad smile. 'But I've got adventures of my own.' She reached out and took Rose's hand. 'Bringing up this one.'

Rose let her mum's hand go and peered up on tiptoes, trying to look through the TARDIS windows, her eyes burning with curiosity.

The same look Donna always had, the Doctor reckoned, back when he and Donna…

'No,' Donna said, easing Rose away. 'Because something will go wrong and you'll end up on Mars. With Chaucer. And a robot shark.' Then she stopped. Was that a memory? 'That actually happened, didn't it?'

'Oh yeah,' the Doctor said. 'But actually I was thinking…' He leaned right into Donna's face and winked. 'We could go and see Wilf.'

Donna knew what he was doing. Dangling a bigger carrot over the initial one. 'Oh, that's cheating,' she murmured.

'Just a suggestion.'

Sylvia jabbed the Doctor's shoulder. 'I mean it, both of you. Don't. You. *Dare.*'

But the battle was already lost. 'Oh but imagine his face, Mum. He'd be *so* happy. All those secrets Granddad kept for years. Things he thought I'd never remember. And to see the Doctor one more time …'

It had to be said, Sylvia Noble knew when she was beaten and retired gracefully. 'All right, then.' She gave the Doctor one of her 'looks', and he actually took a step back – those 'looks' often resulted in a sore face! 'Just one trip,' she said. 'That's all. One!'

And Donna grabbed the Doctor's arm, so excited. 'One tiny little trip! And that's a promise, Mum.' She grinned at the Doctor. 'Like the old days, just me and the Doctor, together and—' She stopped and let go of the Doctor, turning to face her husband, who she only just seemed to remember was standing there. 'Is that all right?'

There was a brief pause that seemed to last hours to everyone else. But Shaun just said, 'Course it is!'

Donna hugged him. 'Well, a lot of husbands would worry. Me. In a box. With another man.'

Shaun shrugged. 'Yeah. But not *him.*'

The Doctor went to respond and then realised he wasn't sure if he'd been paid a compliment or a huge insult. He didn't get a chance to check, as Donna grabbed his elbow.

'C'mon, Spaceman.'

With a smile, the Doctor opened the TARDIS door and walked in, Donna right behind.

* * *

Donna's newly returned memories of the TARDIS interior were vivid, and it never occurred to her that the TARDIS she remembered wasn't what she was going to see walking through those doors.

But it was different. And how.

The TARDIS had always been bigger on the inside than the out but this … this was beyond belief.

It was a perfect hemisphere, which would probably cover most of Wembley football pitch. The roundels were still there but glowing in soft blue pastels. The hemisphere itself, and the floors and walkways, oh so many walkways, were perfect white. It was hard to see where things started or ended.

And it had a scent, sort of minty, to match the glow from the roundels that now made the entire white walls slightly blue too.

At the heart of it was the console, again, in immaculate white, but still covered with insane buttons, switches and dials over its six panels and that central glass column now went right up into the ceiling at the apex of the room.

The Doctor was already running around the walkways and floors, tapping roundels, then dashing back to the console, then off to a doorway on one level, down to another doorway on another level. And he was whooping like a child given its favourite toy on Christmas Day.

'This is amazing,' he yelled to her from one level. 'It changed,' he added running down to another. 'Oh, you clever thing,' he said, this time to the TARDIS itself as he opened a door, peered in and shut it again. Then he made his way excitedly to the console, where Donna joined him. He gleefully pointed at things on the console that Donna knew she could never understand; even so, she found she was caught up in his enthusiasm.

'It's got… this!' he was saying. 'And that! Oh and where's the… Ooooh, what's that?'

Donna noticed that the blue wall glow had given away to a soft green, the roundels illuminating everything like a forest now, and the smell had changed. It was like… eucalyptus oil, woody and fresh.

'Still a bit nippy,' Donna quipped, determined to have the last word, and glad to see her oldest, bestest mate so happy.

'Aww, c'mon,' he pouted and she laughed at his face.

'All right, it's gorgeous,' Donna conceded playfully. 'It's cleaner. It's grown. But I still don't get it.'

The Doctor stopped fussing and gave her a querulous look.

'Okay so the TARDIS can change,' Donna continued. 'But what about your face? Why did it come back?'

'Does there have to be a reason?'

'With your lifestyle? Yes!'

The Doctor shrugged. 'Well, I'm stuck with it now and…' He suddenly saw something on the console and tapped at it. The console gave a little burble and something lit up deep inside it. 'Oh, this is brilliant! It's even got a coffee machine. Do you want one?'

'You're kidding…'

'With cold milk, yes?'

Donna couldn't argue with that. 'You remembered.'

The Doctor tapped something Donna couldn't see.

146

A tiny hatch in the console slid back and a coffee in a white porcelain cup on a saucer rose up on a teeny-tiny platform. Donna reached out as the Doctor passed it to her.

'Thank you,' she said, holding the cup and saucer slightly away from her chest. 'Gotta be careful though. This is how I lost my last job. I dropped a coffee in the computer.'

The Doctor however didn't seem to hear her. He was focused on her comment about him remembering how she always took her coffee. 'I really *do* remember,' he said finally, still trying out new controls. 'Every second. With you. And I'm so glad you're back because it killed me, Donna. It killed me, it killed me.' He finally looked at her and stopped playing. 'It. Killed. Me.'

If she hadn't been holding the coffee, she would have hugged him, he looked so wounded. So apologetic. She knew it wasn't his fault. It had *never* been his fault. He had done what he did to save her life and she could never criticise that, only be grateful.

'But we can have more days, can't we. I mean, why is it always such a big goodbye with you? Why is it "one last trip"? You can visit with my family. We can do outrageous things like ... like have tea! And dinner. And a laugh.'

The Doctor still looked unsure.

'Of course,' Donna continued, trying to cover up the last vestiges of awkwardness the only way she knew how. By talking things to death. 'You've been given a second chance and you can do things differently this time. So why don't you try something completely new, and actually have some friends?'

'Yeah,' the Doctor seemed to be accepting this. 'Yeah.' Then a final, more affirmative 'Yeah!'

'Like look at us right now,' Donna continued. 'Here we are, having coffee. What's gonna go wrong with that?'

She shrugged.

And she remembered that she was holding a cup of coffee.

And she remembered that shrugging and holding cups full of coffee did not go well together.

And the whole contents of the coffee mug sloshed straight into the centre of the TARDIS console.

'Oh my god,' Donna breathed finally. 'I did it ag—'

She never finished the sentence because the Doctor rugby-tackled her and they both hit the deck, just as a huge flame roared out of the central column where the coffee had gone in. If that wasn't bad enough, the glass column thing started moving and she heard the familiar sound of the TARDIS dematerialising. The TARDIS interior was glowing red and the smell ... the smell was really unpleasant, pungent, it reminded her of ... yes Pyroviles, Pompeii, volcanos. Like sulphur or burning.

The Doctor was trying to bat the flames out, but it was no good. The TARDIS was in flight, but not in any accepted use of the word 'smoothly' or 'efficiently' or 'nicely'. It was, frankly, throwing them around in a terrifying fashion.

'What's happening?' Donna asked as she hauled herself up. 'Where are we going?'

'I have no idea,' the Doctor finally answered. 'It's completely out of control.' The whole console erupted in a mass of sparks, sending them both toppling backwards. 'We could end up anywhere in time and space!'*

*You can discover what happens next in *Doctor Who: Wild Blue Yonder*

Acknowledgements
by Anthony Dry, Target cover illustrator

As I take my leave of the Target *Doctor Who* range, I would like to thank the team at BBC Books over the years for their wonderful support and guidance: Albert DePetrillo, Dan Sorensen, Beth Wright, Nell Warner, Shammah Banerjee and Steve Cole. You have been truly great colleagues.

Another big 'thank you' goes to Russell T Davies for giving me this amazing opportunity; to Lee Binding and Peter Ware for their help; to Gary Russell for his ongoing support; and to my partner in design crime, Stuart Crouch, who started me on this journey with my very first *Doctor Who* illustration gig many moons ago. His mentorship, sanity checks and colour expertise help make the covers what they are.

Further thanks go to my wife, Jen, who has put up with the long hours I've worked, and my children, Erin and Joel, who like to 'dot pictures' when I leave my computer unlocked!

However the biggest thanks must go to my parents who have supported me through everything: my mother, Winifred, for her artistic DNA, and to my father, Dave, who always encouraged me to read by buying Target books on his lunch hour in the '80s and who is now not in the best of health.

Love and gratitude to you all.